[handwritten inscription] Cerene x Thankyou for the support!

Dogknife

Liam Rodgers

[handwritten signature] Liam Rodgers

DEDICATION

My beautiful daughter Niamh-Marie Rodgers and son Jupiter
Brice Lewis-Rodgers.

CONTENTS

ACKNOWLEDGMENTS

Mister Quick, editorial services; Raphael Achache, cover design & formatting; Star Lewis, typing.

Without the donations of the following people, via Indiegogo.com, this print edition of Dogknife would not be in your hands! The warmest thanks to everyone who gave money to make this possible (in no particular order):

Maxima; Emily; Rachel Jacobs; James Shearman; Leon Ross; Ruth 'Struth' Heinemann; Janet 'Planet' Heinemann; Elly Valentine; Nell Coulter; Dan Hughes; Star Lewis; Mary 'Grandma' Mclaughlan; Karen Cadogan + Niamh-Marie Rodgers; Cheryl Lewis; Llewella White; Aaron Calladine + Kim Lewin; Matthew Swindles; Alexander O'Riordan; Paul Mark Gaunt; Ezra Alexis Hunton; Charlie Pitt; Laura Girardi; Declan Green; Terrence Green; Matt Pykett; Jane Wright; Jade Baptiste; Karina Nickson; Colleen Desnos; Pamela Crews; Cas Cowlin; Jayne Lipbalm; Sue Weasel; Hollie Flint; Lynn Sidnell; Kirsty Davison + Henry Ephraim Ferris; Jon Maxfield; Rich Close; Janet Savage

Prologue

I1A - Page 2 Police Copy CRN/13145

POLICE INTERVIEW, ROBERT HENLEY...REF:
C10/10/66983

PRESENT: DC ANDERTON, DC HUGHES, KAZAN,
MALDEN AND CO (SOLICITORS) 02/02/99

Officers introduce themselves, followed by:

DCA: Please state your full name, date of birth and current
address.

RH: Robert Henley, tenth of September, nineteen forty-
four, **CENSORED** Road, West Bridgford, Nottingham.

DCA: Thank you.

SOL: Mister Henley's legal representative, John Saunders
of Kazan, Malders and Company, Solicitors of
Nottingham.

DCA: Cheers.

DCH: Mister Henley... Robert...

RH: Yes?

DCH: This is your second interview... Er... Regarding the
alleged rape of Sarah Mellors... Erm, who lives in Radford,
in the early hours of the thirteenth of January nineteen
ninety-nine, also in Radford... Sarah Mellors was assaulted
against her will, which has been previously detailed to you,
to the, errr... Tape. She contacted the police, namely my

colleagues in the anti-vice squad, or erm... The vice team, who in turn mounted an investigation based on the details ascertained by them.

RH: Yes.

DCH: Sarah Mellors states in her statement of the sixteenth of January nineteen ninety-nine that she was walking along Bentinck Road in Radford, approximately at two thirty-five in the morning, of the thirteenth of January nineteen ninety-nine... She was returning from a small gathering at a friends flat at nearby, erm... Hartley Road, the Radford Flats, and she states, and I quote...

RH: Yeah.

DCH: She states: 'There wasn't many people round and there were hardly any cars around and I wasn't really thinking about anything and that's when the car pulled up and I recognised it straight away... It was a new shape Rover...'

(Continued on separate sheet)

I1A - page 3 Police Copy CRN/13145

POLICE INTERVIEW, ROBERT HANLEY...REF: C10/10/66983

PRESENT: DC ANDERTON, DC HUGHES, KAZAN, MALDEN AND CO (SOLICITORS) 02/02/99

(Continued...)

DCH: 'I could tell that it was metallic colour, silver, and I recognised the driver...'

DCA: Then Sarah describes the driver further, stating that he was, 'Podgy', with almost no hair and small glasses.

RH: Mmm.

DCA: She then describes a conversation taking place and an agreement takes place, errr, in her own parlance, an agreement is arranged to do business... In the car, between herself and the driver of the Rover at another location, namely on the Forest Recreation Ground.

DCH: Do you know what the phrase 'do business' means?

RH: I think so, yes I do.

DCH: Can you tell us what it means?

RH: Well, I think it's... She's a prostitute, so it's an arrangement to pay for sex, basically.

DCH: Yes.

DCA: Is Sarah Mellors known to you as a prostitute?

RH: Erm, how much of this is going to be told to my wife?

DCA: Frankly Mister Henley, that's not really an issue that myself and my colleagues are concerned with, we're investigating a serious allegation of rape, of a teenage girl, in a car, on the Forest Recreation Ground.

DCH: This is a gallery of still photographs taken from three separate CCTV cameras, operated by the council, reference numbers PH1B, PH1C, and PH1D respectively, and show a car and a driver, and on this one here...

(Continued on separate sheet)

I1A - page 4 Police Copy CRN/13145

POLICE INTERVIEW, ROBERT HANLEY...REF: C10/10/66983

PRESENT: DC ANDERTON, DC HUGHES, KAZAN, MALDEN AND CO (SOLICITORS) 02/02/99

(Continued)

DCH: The CCTV operators were able to, errr, get a close-up of the number, the number-plate, the registration number actually...

RH: Yes, it's...

DCH: Sorry?

RH: I recognise it.

DCA: Why do you recognise it?

RH: It's mine, my Rover.

DCA: It's your car?

RH: Yes, yes that's me.

DCH: Do you remember driving your car, this car, on the night of the thirteenth of January, at this time and in this area, Bentinck Road, Forest Recreation Ground?

SOL: I think it's established that Mister Henley was there.

DCH: We just need him to confirm.

SOL: I know, but can we... (Inaudible)

DCA: Okay, let's clear this up, cut to the chase, Robert.

RH: Yes.

DCA: In your own words tell us what happened on the night, what you did since early evening 'til the time these were filmed, all your movements as you can remember them.

RH: From the beginning?

DCH: When did you leave your house?

RH: Um... I think about half-eleven... Eleven. Approximately eleven.

DCH: Eleven?

RH: Yes, around eleven.

(Continued on separate sheet)

I1A - page 5 Police Copy CRN/13145

POLICE INTERVIEW, ROBERT HANLEY...REF: C10/10/66983

PRESENT: DC ANDERTON, DC HUGHES, KAZAN, MALDEN AND CO (SOLICITORS) 02/02/99

(Continued)

DCA: And then what?

RH: I um...Left the house and, erm, drove to town.

DCA: Which route did you take?

RH: From West Bridgford... Over Trent Bridge... Onto London Road... Through town... On the one-way system through the city... Maid Marian... Through Canning Circus and basically into Radford...

DCA: To cruise for prostitutes?

RH: Well, I mean, does this get said in court?

DCH: If this comes to court, then yes it will. Just carry on...

RH: Well yes, I was cruising.

DCA: You were kerb crawling.

RH: Yes I was, it sounds sad... I want to say sorry to my wife.

DCA: So you were cruising for what, two, three hours?

RH: Yes, about that yes.

DCH: And at what time did you see Sarah Mellors?

RH: Erm, I'm not one-hundred percent certain, a quarter past two... I saw her at Hartley Road first and then drove up Alfreton Road, and then Forest Road, and onto Southey Street to see her as she walked along Bentinck Road, and that's when I stopped the car because I recognised her.

DCH: Where from?

RH: I'd picked her up before, before that night, yes.

(Continued on separate sheet)

1 Me and Mine

Dogknife is the name of the blade that I had strapped to my right ankle, in case I had to fight a dog and it's the one I used on the punter. I never meant to use it on people; I had it for years because I thought one day I would have to fight a dog, properly fight a dog, to the death. A random Pit Bull or Alsatian would chase and catch me and I'd be there fighting, giving it my left arm to chew, like putting my left arm in its mouth to distract it and then bang! I pull out Dogknife and stab it in the neck until it dies.

Boo Boo Girl said it was an irrational fear, a fear you're not supposed to have, from deep inside ya. I've always adored dogs - that's the mad thing. We had all kinds of dogs when we were growing up. A Jack Russell, a cross Mongrel, an Alsatian, and we once had a Sausage Dog. I like all animals, really. I even like wasps now, and I used to hate them. I never got stung by one, I just din't want to because I thought I'd get anaphylactic shock or whatever it's called. I thought I'd get that and my body would swell up and then I'd die because I couldn't breathe. I saw it on 999, the TV show from years ago, some guy was jogging along the canal and he got stung and he got anaphylactic shock, or whatever you call it, and he fell down with his mouth all swollen and he couldn't breathe. He got rescued in the end, but it's my luck that I'd die from it.

Boo Boo Girl said that was an irrational fear as well.

Valerie said I was just a crazy bitch; but she's nuts, Valerie is. She cut all a girl's hair off in her sleep because the girl owed her money and when the girl woke up bald, Valerie acted like nothing happened.

Boo Boo Girl nick-named her Valerie, after a mad woman who stabbed the weird artist Andy Warhol, Valerie Solanis or whatever she's called, I can't remember her full name. And not many people could get away with giving Valerie a nickname, that's the maddest thing, but Boo Boo Girl did when she first met her. That's what Boo Boo was like, she would meet you and then give you a nickname and it din't matter if you liked it or not because it would stick. Boo Boo always gave nicknames that suited the person, the way they acted or talked.

Boo Boo was the clever one like that, knew how to spell loads of posh words and knew history and all the important stories in the news and what was going on in the world. She was the best looking out of all of us as well, her cute round face, like those porcelain dolls. She gave me the nick name Gizmo, after one of the creatures in the film Gremlins, but not the green and nasty buggers; the fluffy and nice one. My hair gets dead fluffy, it's long and curly, and it feels soft and that's why she called me Gizmo. I like it.

It was dead sad how Boo Boo got her nickname. We were having a session in my room at the hostel, my mates came because I had a quality sound system, which was actually a shit Grundig make, but had good speakers, and everyone chilled out there. The boring lads always wanted to come in, they never had any drugs or loot and knew that we did, so we mainly had sessions on our own until Scott and his safe mates moved in, but we only let them lot in, 'our boys' we called them, if they had draw or billy, or both.

We were there one night, Boo Boo Girl, Valerie, and me; having a session, listening to music and playing crazy-rules monopoly because we'd lost half the pieces. We folded bits of paper as houses, wrote out daft Community Chest cards (like collect a crisis loan from the dole, or rob the bank for three seconds). Valerie had been on the beat and done three punters and raised sixty quid: a good raise for an hour on the beat. That was before I'd gone out at all. Valerie din't give a fuck though, she just went out and came back with sixty pound. We got caned on our own, buzzing off each other and having a laugh. We were all chatting crap about the game, then I goes to Boo Boo, "Ow comes people call ya Boo Boo Girl?'

Her real name's Sarah and I heard her cousins using the nickname when they came to the hostel to visit. I din't say anything when I first heard it, I thought it was cheeky, but after we'd known each other for longer, because we'd been taking drugs together and had a vibe, I thought it was a better time to ask. All three of us were proper mates by then.

Boo Boo said it was a family name they'd called her for years. She looked embarrassed. She might have thought we were going to rip the piss out of her, like when Valerie took the mick out of Boo Boo's posh sounding Nottingham accent; which ain't as posh as the really rich people and that, but was more than mine and Valerie's as we're plain common. In order, Boo Boo was blatantly a bit posher and cleverer, it was then probably me just 'cause I went to school and Valerie din't even go to school after she turned twelve. Valerie had the roughest life of anyone I ever knew.

My room was the place away from all of that, the place for us to be ourselves. When it was us three having a session, we din't like other girls coming in with us and I only let one other girl in, when them lot weren't around, called Tanielle, who I knew from down The Meadows. No-one else in the hostel liked Tanielle or got on with her, I think mainly because she was black and from The Meadows and knew tough people down there, so people were scared of her. We knew some of the same girls from growing up down there and that's why I got on with her. If I din't grow up down The Meadows, I probably wouldn't have got on with her like I did.

After Boo Boo said it was her family nickname she started crying, like really deep. Me and Valerie looked at each other and were both upset. We all cried. We'd never cried in front of each other before. Boo Boo said the only time in her life when she was proper happy was when her dad would call her his 'little boo boo girl'. He'd say, 'Where's my little boo boo girl?' Boo Boo would go running to him and jump into his arms.

We already knew Boo Boo's dad was dead from cancer, everybody in the hostel knew. She went to his grave every now and then, always alone, to put fresh flowers on it. She din't care that people knew, us lot din't say anything except we started calling her Boo Boo Girl to try and cheer her up. It made her smile.

Boo Boo Girl was so beautiful when she smiled, a proper cute face. She had small dreadlocks that she tied back and her fringe was hanging to just above her blue eyes, what you'd say were sparkling blue. Her hair was brown but she used to dye the fringe and bits of the dreadlocks all kinds of colors, the craziest combos. She always looked beautiful. Always. Valerie tried it on with her once and Boo Boo weren't having none if it. Boo Boo was 100% straight. Valerie's bisexual and so am I, but I don't like telling people, I've tried to keep it secret. Valerie don't care who knows and when you look at her, you can tell anyway. I could when I met her; I'm wicked at spotting gays and lesbians.

I first saw Valerie walking into the office of the hostel when I was having my moving in meeting, when you sign all the papers and get ya key and that lot, and I thought, *she's a dyke*. Valerie was wearing a black Nike tracksuit, Air Force trainers and mousy hair in a ponytail. She had gold rings on three of her skinny fingers and a tattoo on her neck, on the right side. The tattoo was SHANNON, her brother's kid. Valerie's tall for a girl and thin. I thought she must be a dyke because she looked like a tom-boy. Valerie gave off the vibe of a girl who you wun't fuck with. Don't get me wrong, I'll fight anyone if I have to, especially other girls, not because I love fighting, I don't, but when you have to fight and that's it, you have to fight. Valerie was one of those girls that I wun't want to fight because I'd probably have to kill her to stop her from coming back.

2 The Hostel

Valerie moved into the hostel because she had literally lived in all the other hostels in Nottingham, even the probation hostels, and Waterloo was the last one for her. Valerie had been on the streets for years, since she got abused by her uncle when she was thirteen and no-one believed her, so she ran away. Her mum got hold of her and beat her up in the street, calling Valerie a lying little bitch. Valerie had been living rough or sofa surfing ever since. Probably me and Boo Boo were the only ones who believed her.

Boo Boo Girl was in the hostel because after her dad died her mum got a new man, and it was within months. Boo Boo din't get on with him and argued with her mum all the time over it. Boo Boo thought she had no choice but to leave.

Apart from our crew, there were about twenty other residents. People moved in and out each week, some staying for months, a few weeks, or even days. The odd one stayed over a year and got their own flat if they din't fuck it up. There were all types. I suppose you'd have called us lot the criminal ones, the druggies and thieves or whatever. Back then I wun't have thought that: we were doing what came naturally to us. Now when I remember, people must've thought we were the rude-girls and rude-boys and probably gonna end up inside or dead.

Most of the residents – and half the staff - din't like me, Valerie and Boo Boo 'cause we worked the beat, took drugs with the money and din't give a fuck what they thought about it. We had to deny it to the dick 'ed ones; otherwise they would have grassed us up. It was none of their business. They reckoned we were slags who din't have any respect for ourselves. They din't understand what it was about. Even though we left them alone, they always had opinions on us, so I stuck to my mates.

There was Martin who I never fancied at all, he was ugly, but I got on with him straight away 'cause we both loved jungle music. They call it drum and bass nowadays. Martin was lanky with a big bush of curly black hair and he had a geeky looking face. He had loads of spots and used to pick them all the time. To be fair, and it might sound shit, he wasn't good looking. Well, for me he wasn't. I was just a friend. In fact, I classed him as a proper friend, even though he fancied me and was protective over me. He was a worrier, always thinking about having no money, his Renault's engine, his jungle tapes or his mental mate Floyd Ferris who was a crack head and always bringing trouble to Martin's door.

Floyd Ferris, who everyone called Ferris, was from Carrington and the one guy in the hostel that nobody would ever mess with, not even Valerie, and not 'cause he done some kind of kung fu when he was younger, but 'cause he had a bit of a screw loose. The reason he was in the hostel was because he burnt down the top floor of his parent's house and they kicked him out. When he moved into the hostel, none of the staff knew he was a crack head, but we all did. He was well known around town because his uncle Richard got in the news for growing weed and getting arrested and told the courts he grew it for medical reasons.

One night we were in Martin's Renault, an old shape jalopy with rust on it and everything, toking weed and cruising 'round Radford and we saw Ferris. Martin stopped and Ferris persuaded him to drive to a house in St Anns, near Elm Avenue. We waited in the car, not knowing Ferris was robbing the place. Martin was pissed off. Ferris put the stash in the car and Martin got a fiver for petrol and that was it. Ferris spent the rest of the money on crack, which he smoked in front of us, sucking it down like it was saving his life.

Martin's life was hard, but he was clever. I think his mum and dad were well off, middle class or whatever ya call it, and Martin had enough of them trying to get him to college and be a goodie-goodie. Martin wanted to ignore his parents, take drugs and listen to jungle, mainly DJ Ellis Dee; he was our favorite. Martin liked to be comfortable, with no stress. He din't do complicated.

He used to say stuff like, 'People need to be shown, Stephanie. It's to do with honour. Lots of people today have got no honour.'

'Forget it,' I told him.

Martin would look at me all serious, really in to my eyes, while I'm sitting on his floor, having a sip of liquor or a toke of a spliff, looking up at him, listening.

'Do you know what I mean by honour, Stephanie?'

He never called me Gizmo.

Martin was always telling me about honour and respect, how important they were, to stand for them when you had to. He went deep on it, saying we shun't live on our impulses, like wild animals, we can rise above that. That's why he was peaceful and din't really want trouble, even though he made out he wanted to batter people that pissed him off, but he never could. He had heart, that's what you'd say. If he could've took over the world or summat mad like that, and his rules were the ones everyone had to live by, then we'd all be living more peaceful than we are now. That's how Martin wanted it to be, everybody getting what they needed and having freedom. He was always dissing politicians. Martin and Boo Boo Girl used to talk about politics all the time, much more than me.

Martin died of a heroin overdose a few years later, that's why I've got a little 'M' tattooed on my right ankle. I was gutted about him being gone, but I'll always remember him and that's what counts.

Amy the Rocker died as well.

Amy the Rocker was a small, skinny asthmatic girl with NHS glasses, long, dry blonde hair and eczema. She always had on a heavy metal t-shirt, Converse trainers or Dockers, and leggings with a skirt over them. Trust Boo Boo Girl to start calling her Amy the Rocker. Amy was proper brainy, easily the cleverest of us in the hostel. She was from down South, dead far though, like Hastings, where they had the big battle and the king got stabbed in the eye. I don't know how she got to Nottingham but she did and she was mates with most of us. Amy called us all rude-girls, but I reckon Valerie was the only one who really was.

Amy the Rocker got hooked on smack a couple of years later and caught Hep' C, then pneumonia, and then one night went over and never came back. I never got an 'A' tattooed on me, though, I don't know why. Maybe I should, but then I'd have to get a letter for everyone I know that's died, and that would be daft: my legs would look like the alphabet. With Martin it was different because he had a good soul, if ya know what I mean, but I still think about Amy the Rocker and her cackle laugh that used to make her cough and curl up in pain.

Gay Mark was a rent boy and that's how he used to get his money for his speed and ganja, which he took all the time. Pills were on the streets then, more expensive and stronger than today's. He loved them as well. Gay Mark came back to the hostel one night covered in blood, a black eye, and his nose broke. Two gay-haters, who were pretending to be punters, attacked him. Mark said he'd let them shag him for twenty quid in the bushes on the forest recreation ground. That's where a lot of renters worked. It's famous in Nottingham for the place to go to find rent boys. The blokes battered Gay Mark when he offered to wank them off to get them started. They went in to a rage and battered him. He was only trying to make a raise, poor bastard. He din't even ring the police because he thought they'd do nothing and tell him he brought it on himself.

That's what they told some working girls, too.

I got punched in the eye by a punter once and he nearly knocked me out. He was one of those that love to hurt a girl for no reason. I was stood on Southey Street, not where I'd normally be, 'cause there were more cars driving up there and turning right onto Forest Road at the time. Nowhere else on the beat was busy. Older girls usually worked Southey Street, and they din't like younger ones like us on their patch. If they had a pimp it was worse, because they could be violent bastards, so when we weren't with Valerie we had to be careful.

This one night I was out there alone. Boo Boo Girl was off visiting some of her school friends and fuck knows where Valerie was. I lay down in some Asian guy's van and did him for twenty-five quid. I told him to hurry up. I'd done him and was stood in short black skirt, black fishnets, black heels - even though I don't really like heels - and a simple black, tight-fitting top.

I was stood at the top of Southey Street, looking up and down, a blue car pulled up, and this bearded guy with black hair and Hawaii shirt nodded at me to walk onto one of the streets off Southey Street. I think it's called Hardy Street; I walked onto it and waited for him to go around the block.

I was like, 'Do you want business, then?' I was leaning in the passenger side giving it all smiles.

He was like, 'How much for a nosh?' Most punters din't use that word: they said blow job.

I said, 'Fifteen quid.' He leaned over and I felt pain and had a white flash in my eyes. I was on my skinny arse before I could take a breath and get my bearings. He drove off and I was sat in the street, dazed as fuck.

A black rude-boy was walking past at the top of the street and he pointed and laughed, 'Slag!' I sat and cried. I din't say anything back.

I got up and walked back to my room, crying all the way, even when I got into bed, crying like when ya whole body shakes and I cried 'til I fell asleep. My cheek was sore and my jaw was stiff. I felt inside-out.

I still went out there the next day though, on the beat. I weren't gonna let no prick scare me off. It wasn't nice getting smacked, but fuck that, I wan't gonna be in fear. Lots of people don't give a shit about working girls, so we took a risk every day we were out there.

Kelly Byrne was found stabbed to death, just near where that idiot punched me. The beat is small, you get to know most faces, so it affects all of us. She'd probably been stabbed by a rapist punter or her mental-case pimp, Roger. A few girls said it was Roger, but no-one will find out because the police din't really give a fuck. A dead girl on the beat: *so what?* That's probably what they're thinking.

Working girls are like therapists, that's how I see it. Boo Boo explains it the best, but it's basically men want sex and women can help them. Like doctors, fixing them. It ain't the whole picture, but it is part of it. Prostitution is about filling in the need for men to get their end away. A few of them are desperate for it, or addicted to sex. One or two of them just sit there talking or offering you a meal or extra money.

Every now and then I'd get a weirdo, one that wants to do fetish or hold a mirror underneath so he can watch his nob going in and out. One punter wanted me to shit on him, on his chest, and he wanted to see it coming out of my bum as he was cumming. I said no and told Valerie.

Valerie rang the guy up and was like, 'Do you want me to shit on you for sixty quid?'

Me and Boo Boo were like, 'Don't do it Val, it's disgusting!'

Valerie laughed, 'Fuck it! He's cleaning it up, not me. All I'm doing is bobbing on him and getting out of there!'

She did it as well.

Most punters just wanted straight sex, though. We lay down and they fucked me. I got the odd wannabe stud-muffin who wants to bend you all over and get you to sit on him and do you up the bum and whatever. With blokes like that I used to make them cum quicker by sticking my finger up their arse when I'm giving them a blow job or make sex noises and pretend to be really turned on. There are all kinds of tricks a girl can do to make a man cum quicker than he wants. And I always had a Johnny on them. I never did it without one. I din't know any girls personally who din't use a Johnny. A few don't. They're usually the bad on it ones, the smack and crack heads, all scabbed up and shit. It's sad really, and I'd like to say that it din't happen, but it did. As far as I was concerned, a punter had to have a condom on or it was no business for him.

When I was growing up all I ever heard about prostitution was bad stories, that prostitutes were dirty and full of viruses and always wanted to have sex with men; that they should be put in prison and have criminal records and it's the worst job a girl could do. I suppose I went along with that like most people, I din't know different, and down The Meadows my old mates threw stones at prostitutes and called them names. I grew up thinking that they were all thick slags with viruses.

I moved into the hostel and met Valerie, the first working girl that I'd known. I was interested in Valerie after I found out she worked on the beat, and getting to know her changed my views on prostitution.

3 On the Beat

Away from school teachers telling me to buck up my ideas, and from my mum and all the stress at home, I din't have to hide my feelings, was free to be myself. I was only sixteen, but felt older, like nineteen. I smoked fags, shagged lads if I wanted, and stole from shops and took drugs. When I moved into the hostel I was my own boss.

I only lost my virginity after I'd moved into Waterloo, but I used to lie and tell people I lost it when I was eleven. I don't know why I lied; I reckon I was embarrassed that most other girls and lads lost theirs when they were twelve and thirteen. Not unless they were lying, too. Probably one or two of them were.

Me, Valerie and Boo Boo Girl were sitting in the front room of the hostel, with the TV on, going twos and threes on a fag and no-one else was around. The big long sofas in there stank of smoke and sweat and other shit, and the table in the middle had a couple of full ashtrays on it, but the nubs had been raided so only the paper and spongy, yellow fag ends were left in a pile. There was nothing on the walls except a sign that said, 'ANY RESIDENTS CAUGHT DRINKING ALCOHOL OR SMOKING BANNED DRUGS IN HERE WILL BE EVICTED'. Other than the brown, piss-stained carpet that you wouldn't even let a scruffy dog sit on, there was nothing else in the room. It was barren, like a typical hostel.

Valerie said she was off to work, stood up and rubbed the creases in her blue boob tube. Her tattoos and gold jewelry and skinny body did make her look a tart, there's no doubt about it, it's not like she dressed like it normally. We knew that she din't dress like that. She loved track-suits and trainers all day long, so when Valerie went on the beat she made the effort. She still kept her hair in a pony-tail, though.

'What's it like Val? Do you enjoy it?' I'd been gagging to ask her about it for weeks. She asked me if I'd had sex.

'Of course I have!'

Val asked me how many times and I was like, 'Three or four.' A lie: I'd only slept with the same lad twice.

Valerie goes, 'Well, was any of them not very nice, or over dead quick and not comfortable?'

'One of them couldn't keep it up properly and spunked on my leg after he pulled it out.'

Boo Boo Girl laughed.

Valerie went, 'Well kidder, most of the time it's like that and you get paid for it.'

In her sweet voice Boo Boo Girl asked Valerie if she felt bad about it.

Val looked confused, not pissed off and said, 'Why the fuck should I feel bad?'

Boo Boo said because it was against the law.

Valerie sat down and went, 'Look,' like she was our mum, sitting on the edge of the sofa, 'men always want to get their ends away. That's a fact. They've got cocks and that's what they do, they can't help themselves. They pay and most of them are nice about it. I'm safe and clean, so where's the stress?'

I said, 'Nowhere, really, I suppose.'

'Exactly, babe,' Valerie said. 'There is no harm. It's a job, I get paid. Sex therapy, ya get meh?'

Valerie left for work, did an hour and earned a hundred quid.

Me and Boo Boo Girl sat there talking. All the scary tales we'd heard about working on the beat, catching viruses, getting arrested or battered, walking the streets of Nottingham when there's robbers and all types of lunatics on the loose, but it was exciting as well. The money to be made was the point.

'Just think,' said Boo Boo Girl, 'we could earn loads

of cash with our looks!'

I said to her, 'They'd be queuing down Alfreton Road for you!' I asked her if she'd ever do it. She bit her bottom lip, glanced away.

'I wouldn't do it alone. Valerie's brave.'

'I know,' I said, 'and she's been doing it ages though an't sheh?'

'Shall we try it Boo?' I asked.

Boo Boo Girl said she would if we got punters together, and din't tell friends and family that we were prostitutes.

We both swore down: 'Cross my heart and hope to die, stick a needle in my eye. I won't tell anyone.'

A couple of days later we were sat in Scott's room, chilling out and listening to tunes, waiting for Scott and the rest of our boys to come back with draw. It was me, Boo Boo Girl and Valerie, sitting and smoking fags. We were having a laugh and I kept looking over at Boo Boo to get her attention, to ask Valerie about us going on the beat. Boo Boo looked at me as if to say, *you ask her!*

I came out with it, 'Me and Boo Boo wanna start working.' Valerie is usually dead quick to say something, but she din't click on straight away.

'Doing what?' She asked.

I go, 'Working.'

'Yeah, I know working,' Valerie said. 'Doing what?'

'On the beat.'

Valerie's eyes nearly popped out, I'm not lying.

'Are you fucking joking?' She looked disgusted at both of us: for some reason mainly at me.

I started to say, 'Well, we want –'

Valerie interrupted me and said, 'Please tell me you two are joking, ya get meh, 'cause if ya are it ain't even funny!'

She stood tall, with her hands on her hips.

'Well?'

Boo Boo goes, 'We want to earn some money Val.'

'You wanna earn money? Get another fucking job then! Dean and them lot are starting telesales next week, go with them if you want money.'

Boo Boo and me looked at each other like scared little girls. Valerie was being our mum.

I had a vision of stabbing her. I don't know where it came from, I was angry I suppose. I started to well up inside, like when boys used to poke my tits and run off in the playground, and I din't understand what the joke was. All I knew was that it made me angry, and I'd kick the boys who did it as hard as I could. It might have been a joke, but when they laughed at me I din't like it, and I started to cry and get mad. I wan't like most of the other girls: take it and go red. My dad told me always to defend myself when anybody made me cry.

I said to Valerie, 'You do it.'

'Yes, Gizmo,' Valerie goes, 'I do it, and that's the whole point of what I'm saying. I've been on the beat for fucking ages, since you lot was at school.'

I reminded Valerie she was only two years older than us and she went red.

'Don't get fucking cheeky Gizmo, 'cause I'll slap ya now!' Her finger was pointing at me and veins in her neck and head were popping up.

I looked away, screwing up my face.

Valerie clenched her teeth. 'What's that look?'

I blanked her.

Boo Boo said summat like, 'We're friends remember, don't be like this.' Her voice was soft and her eyes begging.

Valerie shouted, 'It's her!' She was pointing her finger again. 'Looking like she's summat: like she's going to do summat about it!'

I din't speak or bother looking at Valerie. I din't want to fight her, but I would've done if she hit me. Boo Boo's bottom lip was going and she had tears in her eyes. I'll never forget that look.

'Please you two, please. She's sorry, aren't ya Gizmo?'

Boo Boo looked at me.

'Well?' Valerie asked, crossing her arms.

I could feel Valerie staring at me. Boo Boo was crying and she told me to say sorry. She wanted us to forget it.

I jumped up, went over to the door, opened it, turned 'round and spat, 'Soz, alright?'

'Yeah,' Valerie said as I stormed out.

Boo Boo was tryna ask me to stay in the room.

'Don't go Gizmo.'

Scott and the crew walked past me as they were coming back with the draw, and one of them asked me what was wrong.

'Fuck all!' I wan't in the mood for chatting.

I had proper tears flowing when I got back to my room, and I just lay on my bed trying to fall asleep without Valerie's angry face in my head. As I drifted off I was thinking, *who the fuck does she think she is?*

I slept until it was dark and woke up still pissed off with Valerie. I stared in the mirror and decided to do myself up as sweet as you like. I washed my hair in my manky sink and fluffed it up all around my shoulders. I know I've got decent cheekbones and pouty lips so I put some blusher on my cheeks and gloss on my mouth. I mascara'd my eyes and put on a blue skirt which went to my thighs and just a plain white crop top with no bra. I put white ankle socks on and my white-with-blue-stripe Adidas classics. It was my usual going out stuff. I also had Dogknife stuffed in my trainer.

I was going out there and I din't give a shit what Valerie said. The fact she din't want me to go on the beat made me want to. Even though Valerie was the girl who told me about it, working the beat and everything, I felt she was being against me, like tryna be my parent or some kind of fed.

I had two condoms with me and went out to find a punter. I walked up and down Forest Road and down Arboretum Street, Addison Street, Southey Street, Burns

Street, basically all the streets Valerie had told us about and I had seen working girls on, usually close to corners. I was nervous to stop still, mainly because my heart was pumping and I din't want anyone I knew to see me. That was when I was wishing I'd taken out a wig. My mum lived two miles away down The Meadows, but I was still looking up and down like crazy for her old red Golf, thinking she was gonna drive by and see me. I was walking past other girls, and my heart beat faster when fed cars past slowly and the officers were checking me out. I was scared, but I wanted the money.

All my life I'd been poor, and I'm not even joking, we were poor and money never lasted long. Food, gas and electric were always running out. Food was ate dead quick because we were always hungry, like when my mum went to Kwiksave or wherever, me and my two sisters, Jade and Sebella, would eat all the biscuits, yoghurts, pot noodles and crisps and bread within two days because we'd been hungry all week and wanted the sugary shit first, probably for the rush. Treats din't last long, put it that way.

I was mooching around the beat and probably looking lost like a dog that din't know my way home. I can't remember all the details of exactly where I was and who I spoke to, but I definitely turned a couple of punters down because they scared me. They were in cars and looking at me all dodgy.

The first punter I ever did was a guy who came up to me on foot. I was stood on Hardy Street, at the corner with Mount Hooten, where the tram goes past nowadays, mainly because it was close to the hostel and dark. I was still scared of people I knew seeing me. I din't want people to start cussing me before I'd even started. That would have been bait.

My first punter had blonde hair and was about the same height as me, with a clean face and wore a blue denim jacket. That's all I remember, apart from the feel of his breath on me and his dick inside me. As he approached me he kind of looked over his shoulder to check if anyone was near. My heart was pumping more, but not just because I was scared: also a bit of excitement.

'Are you doing business, love?' He asked.

'Sex, ya mean?' I must've sounded fresh behind the tabs. I went red in the face.

'Yeah. How much?'

'Forty quid.'

'No way, too much.' He started to walk away.

My heart was still racing.

'Thirty?' He stopped and turned back to me.

'Twenty-five.'

'OK,' I said. 'Where?'

'Round 'ere,' he whispered, pointing down Hardy Street towards the houses where students live.

'Alright.'

He din't bother asking my name. I wanted to say: *I'm new, ya know!* I soon learnt that most punters want what they came for and to get the fuck out of there, so they don't get nicked or robbed. Society looks bad on men that go to women for sex, so maybe he was shy as well. Maybe it was his first time, too.

We walked down Hardy Street. It was very dark. The big houses looked creepy and haunted with not many lights on with people being out or in town. Another reason it was dark 'round there is 'cause pimps and working girls used catapults to smash the lampposts so it's darker on purpose. Business could get done more secretly that way. I din't find out until later that more girls got robbed and raped on Hardy Street than any other on the beat. Punters used to get mugged or done over down there as well. It was bleak.

We went onto the drive of a big student house with no lights on except for a frosted window, like a bathroom or toilet. A security light came on and I was extra nervous when the punter grabbed my arm for me to be still. After the light went off we crept into bushes against the wall.

He said, 'Lift ya skirt up then.'

I suddenly felt frightened; I was there with a complete stranger in a dark garden, up against a wall with no-one else around. I remembered Valerie saying she always collected the cash first. I fumbled with my knickers and hitched up my skirt and asked for the money up front.

I felt dead cheeky asking. My voice was shaky and I could see my breath in the cold night, like cigarette smoke.

"Ere. Open ya legs.' He pushed the cash into my hand and stepped closer.

I stuffed the loot inside my left trainer and pulled out a condom, tearing it open quick and reaching out for his nob. It was stiff. He helped me roll the Johnny on and I turned my face away from his and held my breath. I could feel him breathing on my neck and the end of his nob was pushing against me. I was shaking and he must've known I was new. He put a finger inside me which made me tense up because it was cold. He lifted up my right leg and shoved his cock in me, making me grit my teeth.

I'd had sex twice with a lad and it wasn't great, but nothing was ever as uncomfortable and awkward as being humped up against that cold wall on a dodgy street in Radford.

I din't get any enjoyment from him but my fanny was a bit moist, which can be normal anyway. I din't cum or get any tingles from it. I was glad an' all, 'cause I din't feel turned on. He poked his willy in and out of me for about two minutes, then pressed against me as he shot his bolt inside the condom. He kind of jerked and twitched a bit and I hugged him a little, just by habit like ya do when someone's up close to you.

I was relieved I survived my first punter.

I put my knickers back on and he dashed the spunked-up condom in the bushes. We set the security light off again and went down Hardy Street.

He said, 'Thanks,' then walked away.

I ran off in the other direction, happy to have the cash all to myself. I was buzzin', like when ya come up on coke or speed, and I just about sprinted back to the hostel. I got the money out of my trainer and held it tight: a twenty pound note and a fiver.

I kept saying to myself, 'I did it. I fuckin' did it.'

Working on the beat wasn't as bad as I thought it was going to be, and I din't care that much.

I could feel where his nob had been in me, which did feel weird I must admit, but it soon went away and I still had the money. The cash is what counted. Not that I wanna go all posh or anything, but I think the right word is elated. I was elated. Twenty-five quid was loads of money to me back then, especially when ya think there was no minimum wage and I was only sixteen.

4 Crimes

One of my first jobs, what ya might call proper jobs, was measuring spots onto England football tops with a ruler and a piece of chalk, which I then had to pass to an old guy who sewed a badge with three lions on it over the spot. I packed Christmas cards as well, in a warehouse on the Blenheim Industrial Estate in Bulwell. I was paid fifteen pounds per shift. My mates from school would've stuck at some of those jobs for life, and good luck to them and all that, but there was me with twenty-five of the Queen's notes for letting a guy put his nob in me for two minutes. All in all, not including the hour that I walked around shitting myself looking to catch a punter's eye, I got paid for five minutes work.

Before I was working on the beat to get twenty-five quid I'd have had to nick a bag full of meat from Co-op, or rob a car stereo, or just mooch through streets until summat came along. For me, that was a normal part of life. I wan't no master criminal, I mainly robbed other girls, and usually when we were in a gang. That's the first crime I ever got convicted for: street robbery.

Me and two of my old school mates mugged three girls waiting at a bus stop. I punched one of them up because I thought she was getting lippy, and we took six pound off them. I had a criminal record – before the age of sixteen – for two quid. I did it when I was fourteen, and the robbery squad arrested me a week later when the three girls we jacked identified us from CCTV. They arrested me and two others, Tracy and Aaroley, who was with her mum doing shopping in town. Tracy and I were looking to rob some clothes from a sports shop when all these undercover police dived on us, saying we were nicked for robbery. I was fifteen by the time it came to sentencing, so the Judge din't send me down; otherwise he was threatening me with five years.

Girls I knew from down The Meadows got sentences like that for the same crimes. I was lucky, really. The Judge still gave me hundreds of hours in an attendance centre order. I went every two weeks for months, sat and listened to ex-convicts telling us not to do crime and watched videos about not robbing cars. We used to play football and badminton, too. I heard horror stories of jail and din't like them one bit, especially about the food being spat and shat in. The conviction must have had some effect on me though, because I din't do anything really serious for two years.

I was sixteen, a prozzie, and that's how I was going on: making money by opening my legs. I spent most of it on drugs, food and fags, having sessions and raving it up in my room with Valerie, Boo Boo Girl and our lads.

I was having a great time and the hostel staff were trying to get me to go back to school because there were still a few months before my final exams. I actually agreed to it at one point; I wanted the staff to think I was a goodie-goodie. I mainly skived off on Thackeries Lane Park, near Arnold, drinking vodka and smoking. Loads of skivers went to Thackeries 'cause it was close to our shit school, Haywood, which is knocked down now. I was living in a hostel in one of the roughest parts of Nottingham, selling my body, taking drugs, and doing more or less what the fuck I wanted. Living at Waterloo and going to school felt weird, put it that way. I was changing as a young women and school was just the same shit. I even had a Monday book. I din't know anyone else in school who got thirty-seven-pound-fifty from the government for living in a hostel and being classed as homeless. I wasn't like the other girls anymore. I din't fit in, even with my long time mates, a couple of them used to be my best mates, with their going to college and working part time, clubbing and boys, and me with my drugs, walking the beat, crime, and eventually prison. I don't know if people in school knew what was going on in my life at the time. While they were preparing for their final GCSE exams I was walking to school on a speed come-down sipping a can of Red Stripe and getting pissed before lessons. That don't mean other girls weren't going through their own shit in life, it's just I wan't into learning about fractions and whatever, I was a thousand miles away from all that in my head. My life was with Boo Boo Girl and Valerie; school meant fuck all to me.

I left and never went back for the exams. I probably could have passed one, two at a push; they would have been English and Drama. I'll never know anyway, so it don't matter. I soon forgot about my old life, with school and school mates, and home life with my mum and sisters. I worked the beat regular and spent the money on clothes and drugs. If I earned fifty quid from doing two punters, that would keep me going with ganja, speed and booze for a couple of days. At that age, with nothing in my head except the dream of becoming a famous girl rapper, the money in my hand was all that mattered.

Hanging around with other druggies, robbers, and twoccers was like the middle bit of my life, I thought I'd be out of those circles soon enough and onto better experiences. My future was on hold. Really I was going to be a big star, I honestly mean it, I was going places. Everyone said I had talent.

Don't get me wrong, working the beat was not glamorous or anything daft like that, it was rough work, not like Heathrow airport call girls where some of 'em can charge hundreds of pounds per hour. Street work is dodgy, that's what I'm saying, but it is easy money. The most I got in one night was three-hundred pound from about seven punters. I'd get bruises from rough punters who I had to swear at or run away from, I'd cry 'cause of them and wish death on 'em. I accepted it. I was out there, offering my teenage body to men for cash. I had to ride the shit times.

I din't like it one bit when it was crap, I was on one of the roughest beats in the country, in an area with a reputation for being one of the roughest manors in England, 'cause of shootings and killings, and I was surviving it and tryna keep my head above it.

It gets to me some days and I sink down and remember the sweaty faces, cigarette breath, and stinky shirts and fumbling hands of the men who had their way with me. We're all going to have memories that stick. I think back to those as a time that shaped me; the street work, drugs and partying, bitch fights; escaping rude-boy muggers who pointed guns in my face; growing up, getting taller; faces, names, and people, some of 'em dead and buried. Radford, St. Anns and The Meadows; all the memories of how it was before the rape.

5 Aftermath

Boo Boo Girl was a mess, and I mean proper, like you wun't wanna see anybody you loved in that way. It makes you want to kill summat. Not that I want to go 'round killing, but seeing Boo Boo wrecked made me feel murderous.

Boo Boo Girl din't open the curtains in her room for ages. She din't wear make up, wun't even leave her room except to go to the bog. Her blue eyes, which used to be soft and cute, were red and bloated from crying all the time. Her hair wan't washed for weeks, and she only wore grey tracky bottoms and a big blue jumper that Scott borrowed her. It was her favorite top. Boo Boo was a mess and it was heart-breaking.

The first time I spoke with her after it happened was two days later. The whole hostel knew and everyone was mostly shocked and the mood in our crew was shit. Valerie was going mental, slamming doors, having arguments with staff and residents and stressing out. Valerie was pissed off with the men in the hostel talking about Boo Boo and she slapped a lad that laughed about it. From that time, all men were in Valerie's bad books. They were in mine as well.

I was stood outside Boo Boo's door, knocking and wondering if she was going to let me in.

I said, 'Boo, are you there darling? It's Gizmo.'

I gently tapped the door, which had a little spy hole. I knew she was in there: we all did.

'Boo can I come in please, mate?'

Suddenly the latch lock clicked off, the handle went down, the door opened a tiny bit.

It was pitch black inside her room. As if she was reading my mind, Boo Boo Girl told me not to turn the light on.

'It will just give me a headache,' she said, her voice

sounding all fragile.

Tears were already in my eyes and my voice was wobbling.

I said, 'Can I come over?'

My eyes were better in the dark. I could make out the bed. I got to it with my hands out, feeling for her legs and climbing up. Boo Boo whispered for me to hold on and she pulled the covers, a purple double quilt, and waited for me to sneak under and squeeze my arms around her. We both cried, and I can't remember many more times when I've cried like that. I stroked her hair and kissed her forehead. I din't really know what to say. I told Boo Boo Girl that I loved her and I meant it. I kept telling her that I loved her, that I was there for her, that I thought she was a strong girl, a special girl.

We kept crying; for me and for Valerie; for everything in that dark room; away from home; family and normal life.

Boo Boo Girl was saying over and over, 'Why? Why din't I just go home? Why din't I? Why did he have to do it, Gizmo?'

I answered, 'Because he's a bastard and you're special. He's a fucking bastard and you din't know he was like that.' Saying it wasn't her fault probably wun't have helped, so I din't.

Tears made the pillow wet. We fell asleep in each others arms, like a needy boyfriend and girlfriend, people who were married or summat. Boo Boo Girl was asleep before me and I listened to her soft breathing and I was praying, even if gods don't exist, I was asking them to protect her from the nightmare. Hopefully sleep was protecting her. I was there, that's for sure, holding her, promising myself I would always be there to make Boo Boo safe from that day on.

By the time morning came, we'd kicked off the covers 'cause we were hot in our clothes, still holding each other. We woke up at exactly the same time, kids were playing outside, or the bin men were out there making noise, so we opened our eyes together.

Boo's face was grey, instead of the usual pink. I stroked her face again. I could see she was suffering, like a wounded angel; the torment was in her eyes. I was taking the pain on as well, getting depressed with my own thoughts, remembering the tough times growing up in The Meadows. None of my mess compared to the dark place Boo Boo was in, I can tell ya, but I was down there, feeling all the discomfort and sadness. I don't know what it's like to be raped, but the stars in Boo Boo's eyes were gone. The skip in her walk was no longer a part of who she was. She din't wear cleavage tops anymore, or mini-skirts. She din't laugh or sing songs with silly words in. And she never worked the beat again.

That morning I managed to get Boo Boo Girl out of the hostel and across town to Arnold Market, to get bits-and-bobs for us. We walked downstairs, and Kissian and Scott were in the hallway beat-boxing and rapping, they stopped when they saw us. They looked at Boo Boo and she ignored them. I glared like I was saying, *get out the way and say nothing!*

As the front door opened, Scott said, 'We hope you're alright, Sarah.'

I said, 'See ya later.' Kissian was giggling as the door slammed behind us. Not all the lads were mature enough to get it, but at least Scott din't say anything stupid.

Boo was crying as we walked to Alfreton Road to catch a taxi, so I put my arm 'round her. We caught one outside KFC and told him to drive to Arnold market. We both sat in the back, me behind the driver and Boo Boo Girl to the left, up to the window. She was watching the world go by and I held her hand while trying to avoid the driver's stare in the mirror. If he'd have known what had happened maybe he wun't have been such a letch. We got to Arnold, paid the pervert driver and spent about an hour getting shopping. I had seventy quid, mainly because I was still working, if ya can believe it, but I was always out there by then. We walked slowly 'round Boots, Wilko's, C&A, an off licence to get some fags, and a couple of charity shops. We went to Sainsbury's and got munchies like frozen pizzas, fish fingers and bottles of pop. Food that's cheap to buy, easy to cook. In one of the charity shops I tried to make Boo Boo laugh by trying on a granny dress, a blue one with massive white flowers on it, like summat a granny would wear, and Boo Boo just smiled with a sigh. I know all she was thinking about was what that bastard did to her. A couple of times we stopped and hugged and she started crying again. Words sounded stupid, like it din't make sense to say ote, so I cuddled her and stroked her hair. Boo Boo trusted me and that was needed. I was there for her, one-hundred percent.

We got back to Radford and Valerie was sitting on the steps next to the back door of the hostel, smoking a fag. Valerie gave us both a hug and kiss on the cheek. She held Boo Boo Girl for longer. Valerie usually din't hug anyone. With Valerie and Boo Boo, I suppose all three of us, it was deep. Val was abused by her uncle and all the horrible memories were back after what happened to Boo Boo.

We went upstairs to Boo Boo's room. I cooked the pizzas and frozen chips and we talked quietly. Boo Boo's room was like any other small room. It had a basic carpet with fag stains and beer stains and puke stains, but it was clean compared to half the other rooms. Below the window was Boo Boo's single bed, with the double purple quilt over it. There were posters on the white walls, which were also marked with lots of pen scribble here and there, and basically just not as clean as a hospital, put it that way. Hostels are always shitty, because people don't give a fuck if they mess up the room or not, it's not theirs to care about. The pictures covering the mess on the walls were of footballers and rock 'n' roll stars. Boo Boo liked football players because they were fit, and rock stars because they were out there and crazy. She enjoyed the music we liked, like hip hop and jungle, but she had her own tastes as well. Boo Boo din't have much furniture except a bean bag with the names of chocolate bars painted on it, like Twix, Bounty, and Snickers and all that lot, and a random wooden chair from the hostel's dining room. She had a table, like a plain, class-room type one, with all her clothes folded on it and most of her bits of tat on there. She din't have a wardrobe or any drawers. Items like Boo Boo's midi system, her box of photos and letters from ex-boyfriends, and perfumes, her purse and what-not on the floor next to the bed. The room also had two hobs attached to the side where the sink was, which had cupboards for food and an old fridge next to it. That's the way it is when you live in those shit holes, but people make do.

Valerie was on the chair, I was on the bean bag, and Boo Boo was in her bed, sitting up against the window with the pillow behind her back. She managed a slice of pepperoni and a few chips. Valerie ate all hers, and so did I. Valerie started skinning up a spliff and Boo Boo looked over at me and goes, 'Do us one of your raps Gizmo, it will distract me.'

I smiled at her. 'Alright babes.'

'Yeah Giz, do the one about it's hard for us, I like that one,' Valerie said. 'It's wicked!'

Because I was with my two best friends I wasn't embarrassed: I sat there, closed my eyes and took a deep breath.

'It's hard out there for us, when we're growing up, it's hard out there for us, 'cause people don't give a fuck, it's hard out there for us, 'cause society doesn't care, so it's hard out there for us when people come to stare and the boys call us slappers, the government tries to trap us, so we wait in the rough streets for change, but fuck all ever happens, they tell us we're born to breed, to grow up quick and have some babies, but we wanna be ladies, when it's not all pink dresses and daisies, it's not all houses and cars, we've got dreams beyond stars, cause we're women from Venus and all the men are from Mars!'

Boo Boo Girl said it was great.

Valerie agreed and went, 'You should be on telly mate! How you make them up, it's fucking dan!'

That's what it was like for weeks: me and Valerie working a few punters to keep us in the shit we needed and help Boo Boo through the aftermath of what that nonce did to her. The staff left us alone to get on with it, and then we started hanging around with the lads again and getting on like we used to. Scott, the tall and skinny one, started getting closer to Boo Boo Girl and they used to go off for walks with their arms around each other. They din't have sex, 'cause Boo Boo couldn't get on that level with men at the time. Scott was there for her like her best male mate and she felt safe with him. If he offered to go with her somewhere, she usually took him.

As time went by, Boo Boo started to cope better, and even went home for dinner a couple of times with her mum and her mum's new husband. They were obviously devastated that Boo Boo was raped, but they never pressured her to move back in with them. As far as Boo Boo Girl was concerned, the same as me and Valerie, we'd left home for good.

We were on housing lists for the Council, and wotcha-call-'em? Housing associations. Valerie was the first in line for a flat because she was the oldest. As long as we din't get booted out and din't leave on purpose, then we'd get offered a flat when we were eighteen, as long as we could handle it with the bills and all that. It was a good set up, though.

All while this was going on, just as Boo Boo was coming to terms with being raped, the police were preparing the case against the punter that did it. Boo Boo was terrified of going to court and when her time came she was literally shaking and crying a lot more, like after it first happened. Our crew packed out the court room to support Boo Boo and to get a look at the monster that did it.

They put up a screen in the courtroom so he couldn't see Boo Boo, so she din't have to look at him when giving evidence. When I first saw him I was shocked because he din't look scary or menacing. He looked pathetic, small, bald and fat. He had thick, pervert glasses and a white shirt and black trousers. He was greasy, and even though I recognised his face from when he was cruising I was glad I never had a memory of his nob inside me. I'm sure I would have remembered him.

By then I'd been on the beat for a year and done hundreds of punters, mainly in bushes and on benches, in the backs of cars. Now and then it would be a hotel, dirty flat, or house in the manor. I was what-do-ya-call-it? Immune. I was immune to it, desperate husbands, boyfriends, and randy builders, teachers, solicitors, and the odd copper. And the weirdos, like the guy who gave me a love bite once, which pissed me off good style for a few days. Fucking idiot. One or two girls get done over nasty every now and then. In a fucked up way, Boo Boo Girl was lucky to not get killed. What I don't understand is why some men treat working girls like scum, like they're not real women, who they can kill and that's it, there's note wrong with it. To think it could be anyone's husband or son, going out and battering prostitutes and going home and acting all normal, like nothing's happened, like they ain't just smashed a girl's head in with a hammer or summat. Those men are out there, sitting on the bus on the way to work, in their uniform, or in the office or in the car, driving to a stuffy business meeting or to pick up the kids from school, and they don't have signs round there neck saying, 'I kill women' or, 'I raped a prostitute last night.'

Ask yourself, next time you see a man walking down the street, *is he one of them?*

Boo Boo said it was because men wanted power

over girls and to be the boss of another human. She said it was mainly because they had empty lives. They take power over a woman, or like Boo Boo, a teenage girl. They are weak men, basically. They are pathetic. They can do terrible shit to innocent people.

When I looked at Boo Boo, I saw beauty, cuteness and a person who's clever and going places, but when I looked at that scum bag, his bald sweaty head and his NHS glasses in front of his pervy eyes, I just saw a petty man, a weak creature. I saw a man who had nothing except that he terrorised an angel who only wanted to help him out to start with. Fucker. I'm not usually a girl who hates people, but I hated Robert Henley with a fashion.

Our crew packed out the court room and he was sat there on his own, billy-fucking-no-mates. The Judge told us to hold it down and not make a noise and all that lot, but we swore a few times and shouted at Robert Henley, then behaved because Boo Boo's mum asked us to. We were all brewing, put it that way.

Dear Robert,

Naturally the boys do not understand why you are not around anymore, or to be exact, why you no longer live here. Please telephone Matthew, he misses you dearly.

As they have never met Janice, and probably never will, I said she'd fallen ill and that you have had to move in with her. I hope you appreciate how much it pains me to lie to the boys in this manner. I shall tell them the truth after the trial, regardless of the outcome.

You must also understand that I can never allow you to live in this house again, as our 'special connection', as you once named it, has gone and that's it. The pain at the moment is close to unbearable. I'll get through it for my sake and the boys. I have no choice. As for you Robert, I love you, but I do not know you anymore. The man you have transformed into these past three years is not the same man I married. I love you for being the father of our two beautiful sons, they love you and so it is up to you to arrange and build your own relationship with them after the trial and prison, or wherever this leads. I still cannot believe this is happening, it is heart-breaking to say the least. I cannot continue this letter, goodbye Robert and I pray that God is with you.

Barbara.

6 Bridgford

He was found not guilty.

It was in the papers saying that Boo Boo confessed to taking money for sex, and that she said she'd been raped to get attention. Well the post was lying and I saw with my own eyes how journalists can write bollocks.

On the witness stand Boo Boo always admitted to being a working girl and walking the beat and all that, and she obviously said she got in the car with a payment for sex but then he raped her. They twisted it in court and called Boo Boo a liar, said she couldn't be trusted because she smoked drugs and broke the law and ran away from home and sold her body for sex. It was horrible to watch Boo Boo Girl on the stand getting treated like that. Valerie was dragged out of the court room for kicking off after the jury said he was not guilty and she shouted, 'Ya fucking nonce case!'

I cried with Boo Boo in her mum's car all the way back to the hostel. She locked herself away again and was even more depressed than she was before because now half of Nottingham knew about it.

When you've grown up in countries like this, you always expect the truth to come out and for life to work out for you when bad shit happens. You think that the authorities - like the courts, social services, the dole, the hospitals, the police, the banks and all the people in control - will get to the bottom of harsh situations and be on your side. The side of truth or whatever, but it isn't like that.

A man can rape a girl and because she's a prostitute then she's treated as if she deserved it, or in some fucked up way asked for it. If Boo Boo had been a Catholic nun or the Prime Minister's daughter, then the whole wide world would have gone mad. In the real world of the hostels, street corners, and shitty housing estates, life isn't fair, so you grow up believing what the teachers and the nosey neighbours say; that the authorities are there for you, to support and help you. Then you realise you're a whatch-call-it? A burden. You realise you're a burden to the system, and that it's against you and you're just slogging it out, desperate to not drown in the fuckeries. And everyone's got their own mess. These are the things Boo Boo Girl told me and I believe them.

I din't trust the police even more after that bastard got acquitted. I din't trust the courts and I definitely din't trust journalists. It did my head in and I started to do nutty shit like throw beer bottles at cars with men driving, and spray graffiti on phone boxes and buses saying ALL MEN ARE BASTARDS or I HATE MEN. I got those ideas from Valerie because she really hated men with a vengeance. She said that's why Boo Boo's rapist got away with it, because the world is ruled by men and it was all men in the court like the Judge and the prosecution. Men prosecutors, men police, men Judges, men journalists. Valerie laughed about the fact the only woman in the court even looked like a man. It's a man's world, that's what Valerie was on about. It started to get to me, put it that way. I wanted to do something about it.

Boo Boo had started to get out and about. Still, everyone could tell she'd changed. I used to be the mate telling her she was special, she'd make it in the world, she had talent and it was her destiny. Afterwards I'd nick a small bottle of Vodka from ASDA on Hyson Green and walk around on my own, crying and being vexed at people on the pavement and willing them to fuck with me so I could start arguments.

One day, a small, old black woman had spilt a load of washing up powder outside the launderette in Forest Fields and people were treading in it and getting it on their shoes. I wun't give a shit about stuff like that usually, but I was pissed and angry.

'Why don't you clean that up?' I said to her, when

she was stood outside having a fag.

'Why don't you?'

I screamed back at her, 'Why don't you shut you're fucking mouth you old bat!?'

'Why don't you!?' She spat. Even the old people in Nottingham have venom.

I went to punch her, raising up my fist, but I din't do it. I wanted to, though. I think back to it now and feel guilty as anything. I'd love to apologies to that old woman, which is mad really, 'cause I've pissed off hundreds of people. It's the ones that you remember that teach you lessons. Back then though, I din't give a fuck. I was heading straight for it, like countdown to the big one. It was always going to happen, like a destiny thing.

I'd not really thought that revenge was real, that it could actually be done. I just fantasised about violence and getting my own back. It was when I was at the Trent, I'd cried all the way down the canal from Station Street, it became obvious – Robert Henley was only up the road.

I was drunk, tears rolling off my cheeks, cussing the whole world to fuck. I'd already clapped a small bottle of Vodka, the 75cl ones, in the morning, so I was pissed by the time I traipsed through The Meadows to the Trent Embankment.

I started under the toll bridge, where ten years before, when I was a small girl and searching for adventure every time I left the house, me and Deidre Pykett dragged a telescopic fishing rod from the shallow part of the river. We used twigs to pull it closer to the edge then grabbed it and started pretending we were fishing, like the blokes we always saw during the season, along the banks. It had a reel, but we din't have bait. We still cast it out with stones and bits of twig on the end. For some reason, Deidre chucked it back in before we had to go home. I din't know why, she just threw it away from the shallow bit and it sank quickly, another adventure over.

I stood there pissed, remembering me and my old

mate Deidre Pykett. I was thinking that telescopic rod was still down there, covered in mud, under the mucky water, that you wun't wanna drink or swim across, even if you were thirsty as a bastard or running from police. I stared at a small girl feeding ducks and geese at the rivers edge. She was screaming in happiness, and I mean screaming, in heaven, with her parents stood nearby, laughing her head off when the animals flapped their wings and quacked 'cause they were fighting for every scrap of bread she dashed.

I wanted to be that little girl, loved and adored, with not a worry in the world. I din't want anything bad to happen to her. I hoped she was going to be free from stress and grief when she was older. Maybe now I think different, that we're all fucked up at some point, but that very moment, as I slumped along the path next to the water, head down with tears splashing on the floor and my eyes red sore, I wanted that little girl to feel no pain ever.

When I got to Trent Bridge, I sat down. It was summer and the sun was bright over the city. People everywhere. Couples in love, families on a walk. A few loners like me, each of 'em doing summat, drinking, smoking or reading, dotted around on the steps that run down to the edge of the Trent, the ones that get covered when it floods. A gang of rude-boys, with BMX's at their feet, stood under the bridge and smoked a spliff and beat boxed. Usually, when I wasn't depressed, I'd go over and rap in front of them and they would be amazed, but then one of them would ruin it by tryna get off with me or pester me for a blow job. Lads are so predictable. The more outgoing and friendly I am to them, the more the studs think that what I really want is a shag and a dick shoved in my mouth. As if cock is all girls think about. Yeah, right. Stood with my eyes red raw and my jaw tense and tight, the only thing I'd have been doing to a willy was biting the fucker off. I wondered what those four or five rude-boys would do to me if they had their way. Treat me like a piece of meat, grabbing and pulling and twisting and lifting, to make them happy. Not all men are like that, but boys aren't men. And men that are pigs are worse than boys who don't understand their own power. That's what Boo Boo told me. Men are supposed to know. Robert Henley was supposed to know.

I could see the handle of Dogknife sticking out of my Adidas and I reached for it. I twisted it to catch the sunlight. My heart raced and butterflies were fighting in my stomach. My tears had dried, anger was building up. I moved the blade, the sun flashed in my eyes. That's when it came to me, like the sun had blinked the idea into my head or summat, like a light bulb going on and you can suddenly see what's in front of you. I was only minutes away from West Bridgford.

I got up and flicked away the blade; put it in my back pocket and walked quickly down the Trent towards the suspension bridge. I got to it and walked across the wooden slats, where I used to hold on tight to the side when I was little because I thought the wood was going to snap. Even now I have dreams where the bridge breaks in half.

I'm stood in West Bridgford, wotcha-call-it? Behind enemy lines. I'm clocking all the silver Rovers, looking for Robert Henley, swearing out loud I'm gonna kill the cunt when I see him; laughing at freaked out and pissed off drivers watching me dash across the road and back again. I was on a mission. I din't have time for treating people politely. I shouted at drivers who beeped me as I made my way around the streets, 'Fuck you!'

The streets look the same in West Bridgford; long with big, leafy trees and nice cars and massive Georgian and Victorian houses and all that. Girls like me stand out like a sore thumb in West Bridgford, especially that day when I had my black hooded top on, pulled up, on a summer's day. The bumpkins 'round there din't scare me though, being from the city gives you the edge over the out-of-towners.

I cotched at one end of the road where the Evening Post said Robert Henley lived with his family. You wun't think they'd print it, but they did. You look and you'll see it. They print people's names and addresses all the time. They din't put the number. I din't need it anyway, I was just gonna clock all the cars and wait for a silver Rover and that bald bastard driving it. I even had some of the number plate memorised, 'cause Boo Boo Girl got it from the paperwork for the case. All I had to do was wait it out. I walked up and down the street, clocked every car, a few silver ones, but no Rover or Robert Henley.

I was there for hours and only went home when I was sober and hungry. I got back to my room at the hostel and fell on my bed, knackered from the walking, anger and stress. I went to sleep quick and slept for summat mad like ten hours.

I returned to West Bridgford the next day. It was like an obsession. I din't even change my clothes. I walked through town, through The Meadows, to nick a bottle of cider under my top from the CO-OP in the precinct, then across the suspension bridge again into West Bridgford. Pissed up. Watching all the cars, looking for the silver Rover. I must have looked scruffy as anything 'cause I'd slept in my black hooded top and blue jeans. I din't even take my creps off when I went to bed, so my feet were dead sweaty. I was stood around, drinking cheapo cider, with my hair greasy. I din't care though, I wan't there for the show or to do a punter, but I must have looked scruffy. Coppers drove past, staring at me, and I saw 'em in time to stash the liquor behind a wheelie bin and Dogknife in my knickers.

I wanted Robert and kept going over in my head what I was gonna do, what I was gonna say, was I gonna rob him or juk him or batter him with a bottle. I ended up plonked down at a bus stop, pretending to wait for a bus that was never gonna come, so I din't look too dodgy to anyone that was clocking me. People call thinking like that street-wise. Maybe it ain't street-wise, more survival, when ya come from a background of mainly having fuck all for most of ya life. Survival, like animals in the wild that have their tactics for staying alive each day, making sure that they don't get took out, the next meal is the most important part of the struggle.

You don't call a fox street-wise. You say it's surviving. The fox doesn't break laws and there ain't any government or police to tell it, *this is right and that is wrong: you can eat wild cats, but not caged hens*. The fox is surviving; it don't see the hens in the cage as right or wrong, it's just a thing in the way of it's next meal, and food for it's kids, cubs, whatever. Is some fox going to stop and think, *is it right or wrong for me to chase this rabbit or cat, catch it, kill it and eat it?* Is it fuck! It's going to catch and eat it. There ain't a fox god, sitting on a cloud, looking down and going, *I can't believe that fox killed another animal, I'm going to punish it.* The fox doesn't get punished. It kills and eats and survives. If it din't, it'd be dead. Not that I'm trying to be some clever philosopher or summat. Some of us are surviving more than others, that's all I'm saying.

I was stood at the bus stop, clocking all the cars, whispering, 'Come on ya bastard, show ya self!' After a while I cried, but I was mainly angry. When I thought about what I wanted to do to him I'd get adrenalin rushes. I wasn't thinking about getting caught, about the police or prison, and all that. I was dreaming of the excitement of the violence I was going to inflict on him. I wanted to fuck him up badly. I got a rush off the thoughts, there's no doubt about it. I'm not a psycho' or anything, like I wanted to stab a stranger for no reason whatsoever. That fucker raped my mate. Simple as that. It could have been me, when ya think about it. It coulda been. That's the point, other girls out there do get raped and all other shit happens to them. Where's their revenge, eh? Where's their wotcha-call-it? Justice: where's their justice?

I went back and stood at that bus stop in West Bridgford three days in-a-row, hoping like mad to see Robert Henley, and it was tiring me out. I couldn't figure out why I din't see him at all. I needed others to help me. Martin, my mate, was the first one I thought of. And Valerie. Then I said to myself, 'Fuck it, I'm gonna tell Boo, Valerie, and Martin, and get a proper plan together.'

7 The Plan

'I'll do it,' Valerie said.

We sat in Martin's jalopy Renault, which was a shitty brown colour inside and out. It had a decent engine, other than that it was a crap car. No heating, no electric windows. No frills. It din't even have a radio, so Martin hooked up a walkman to a car stereo speaker. The sound was tinny, not very loud, like you'd hear nowadays when kids play their phones on the bus. It was tunes though, we made do. Valerie and Boo Boo in the back, me and Martin up front: him behind the wheel. We were parked outside the back of the hostel waiting for a weed dealer called Germaine to drop off a tenner's worth of skunk before we went for a cruise.

Boo Boo din't say anything at first, she listened to us.

Martin went, 'I'm not sure, ya know girls, it's some serious shit.'

Valerie goes, 'What he did to Boo Boo was serious shit and he needs payback.'

Martin was like most boys and blokes: intimidated by Valerie.

'Yeah, yeah. True. He does need payback,' he said.

I said, 'You could drop us off Martin, then pick us up on the other side of the suspension bridge.'

Valerie was nodding.

'We'll run from his house to the bridge.'

Martin bit his bottom lip, looked away and goes, 'I don't know.'

Valerie told him he din't have the balls to do it.

Martin spun his head around towards Valerie, but din't look at her, just down his nose, like he wan't staring at anything.

'Valerie, actually, I have got balls right, it's just big trouble if we get caught, that's all I'm saying.'

'So that's why you can help us babe,' I said, treating him sweet even though he could tell I was doing it on purpose. I shun't have been like that with him, 'cause I know he had a soft spot for me.

I knew that most men will do what you want if you keep them sweet. If a guy, a boy or a bloke, thinks he's in with a chance of putting his nob inside ya, he'll pretty much do anything. By calling Martin babe, I was making him feel sweet. It's like I was saying, do this for me, 'cause I'm your girl. Women learn these little tricks. Boo Boo said it comes from psychology, when we grow up with our dads and the relationship we have with him. Most girls can wrap their father around their little finger, that's where it comes from. Guys who aren't related to you will fall for the same tricks, too, like Martin was doing when I put my hand gently on his thigh.

'Please Martin?' I looked at him with a smile and he looked back all serious.

'Go on Martin,' Valerie said.

There was a knock at the window and we all jumped.

Valerie shrieked, 'Fuckinell!'

Martin span round: Germaine was at the window, sat on a mountain bike. He was dressed in black and had a hooded top pulled up, a black bandana over half his face, with just his eyes poking out. He looked dodgy as fuck. Definite pullers if the coppers saw him.

'What ya sayin' Martin? Did I scare ya?' Germaine's voice was squeaky. He glanced at us lot quick and raised his eyebrows, 'Ladies!'

'Eh up, Germaine,' we said.

The deal was done and Germaine was gone, off to hustle weed on the backstreets of Radford.

Martin goes, 'Wanker!' We chuckled.

Martin threw a lump of cling film onto my lap. He told me to skin up, started the car, and we drove out of the area. As Martin maneuvered down Mount Hooten, along Gregory Boulevard, and onto Mansfield Road towards Sherwood, I peeled open the cling film and inside was a bright green clump of Northern Lights. The smell was hypnotic and filled the car rapidly. I put the Rizla together.

Jungle pinned out of the speaker as we drove past the shops in Carrington and Sherwood, the Peugeot garage and the Robin Hood pub, each of us lost in our own thoughts. Martin was chewing his lip. Valerie was re-doing her pony tail and Boo Boo Girl was staring out the window. It was dark, but there were still people milling about between the pubs, chippies, and taxi ranks.

We said nothing, and by the time we got to Arnold the spliff was lit.

'Three drag pass,' Valerie said.

I took my three pulls, long and full, deep into my lungs. I passed the joint to Martin and he took three long drags same as me.

'That's a nice head, Steph,' Martin said as he exhaled, passing the zoot to Valerie. Val took her three drags same as us and passed it on to Boo Boo Girl. Boo asked Valerie for a blow-back, so Val took the spliff again, turned it around, put the lit end in her mouth. Boo Boo cupped her hands up to Valerie's and sucked hard as Valerie blew, making sure she kept the thick grey smoke going deep into her lungs like me, 'cause we knew it got you stoned quicker. The joint came back to me and I had my pulls and passed it on, and it was like that for a few more minutes until Martin puffed on the roach like a madman, wound down his window, and flicked the nub out.

By the time the buzz kicked in, we were well out of Nottingham and heading for Clumber Park, winding roads and darkness and the odd scrap of light that lit up villages or random houses. Martin liked getting away from the city and parking up with no-one around. At night the car park at Clumber was the perfect spot, so we pulled in there. Martin turned the ceiling-light on and grabbed cans of Stella from underneath his seat. He passed one to each of us and cracked one for himself. Boo Boo passed hers to me and told me to save Valerie twos on it. We sat there tapping our feet and bopping our heads to the drum and bass, sipping our lagers and not really saying much. Martin was skinning up again, one of his seven-sheets: using a whole fag, most of the draw, and guaranteed to get you red as fuck.

Boo Boo Girl said, 'Robert Henley doesn't live there anymore,' her voice was flat, like always when she spoke about him, 'his wife kicked him out before the court case. My solicitor told me on the last day of the trial that he's living in a hotel somewhere in Nottingham.'

Martin was crumbling skunk and tobacco onto Rizla leaves in his lap.

'We could still locate him,' he said.

Valerie asked how.

'Telephone every hotel in Nottinghamshire.'

Valerie laughed.

'Yeah, right. What if he din't use his own name?'

'True,' answered Martin, 'but he probably did use his real name. He wouldn't be expecting any kind of revenge,' he licked the Rizla and rolled the spliff whole, bit off the end of the joint, reached for his lighter, 'because he got away with it.'

'You're going to ring every hotel in Nottingham?'

'It could work Val,' I said, tryna back Martin.

Through the thick, grey ganja smoke that was blazing from his mouth, Martin said, 'It's either that, or we wait outside all the hotels and see if he turns up, and that would take ages. I don't mind ringing them.'

'I'll ring some,' I said.

'There you go,' Martin was jolly, 'that's half of them rang. What you saying Valerie, you gonna ring some?'

Valerie said she thought it was daft and was gonna cost loads to ring the hotels up.

I went, 'We'll raise that easily.'

Valerie frowned.

'You can!'

Martin and Boo Boo said they would put money in.

I goes, 'We could use the phone in the office at Waterloo, when it's film night or a house meeting.'

Martin shook his head.

'We'd have to get the keys and if it was house meeting we'd have to be there.'

'True,' I said.

Valerie whispered, 'We could sneak in through the window when they're watching the film.'

Boo Boo said they always lock the office when it's film night.

'I've seen them doing it.'

'Same here,' Martin said, passing the jay to me.

I was like, 'Fuck's sake!'

Martin said we were getting carried away.

'It's not going to cost that much! There can't be more than a hundred hotels or whatever, at ten or twenty pence a call, what's that?'

'Tenner,' Boo Boo said.

'See what I mean? Ten, twenty quid at the most.'

'That's nothing,' I said, giving the joint to Boo Boo.

'Exactly,' Martin agreed.

'We could use a phone box,' Boo Boo said.

I told them I'd nick a phone book from the library and Martin says, 'Just copy the numbers down.'

'We could use the pay-phone at the YMCA,' Valerie said.

We were getting excited; rushing to come up with answers as the drink and ganja was buzzing our imaginations. It was great to know that Boo Boo Girl wan't against the idea. If she'd have said no, then we wun't have bothered. I might have done summat on my own, but we wouldn't have done ote as a gang. That's why we were buzzing, planning it like a real gang, going over the ideas again and again. It took us a few days to sort our acts out and get on with it.

Boo Boo and me went to the library in town, the big one on Angel Row, and sat with the Yellow Pages and Thompson's and a couple of Evening Posts. We wrote out the numbers all day, I mean, we were there all day 'til it closed. By the time we'd finished I had a massive head-ache and Boo Boo was starving. We went to KFC. We had the phone numbers of all the hotels and B and B's in Nottingham, including the bumpkin areas. It knackered us to get them, but we had 'em. We felt like detectives, trackers. I suppose we were like hunters really, tryna get the what's-it? The scent: hunters trying to get the smell of the prey.

Martin did all the speaking on the phone, and we used one down Sneinton instead of one in Radford, because we thought it was too hot. I gave Martin loads of A4 pages with the numbers on and him, Valerie and me, squeezed into the phone box to start calling. Boo Boo waited in the car.

Martin was like, 'Good morning, can you put me through to Mr Henley, please?' He looked at us and whispered, 'They're just checking,' then he was like, 'you're sure? Okay, sorry about that, thank you.' Robert Henley wasn't there.

Valerie read out the numbers, I tapped them in, and Martin waited for the hotel receptionist to answer.

'Okay, sorry.'

Then another one: 'Thanks anyway.'

And another one, 'Okay, cheers, sorry for that.'

'Thanks anyway.'

'Okay, bye.'

It kept on like that for ages, calling here, there, and everywhere. It started to get stuffy in the phone box, so me and Valerie left Martin to it and sat in the car to skin up. After we'd shared the spliff, Valerie got out the car and went to help Martin. I stayed with Boo Boo Girl for a bit, feeling stoned and talking about what we were going to do and whatever. I remember Boo Boo crying, we were used to it by then so I let her get on with it. The more she got upset, the more my anger and hatred grew. I saw images of Robert Henley in my head: I'd be smashing his podgy, specky face with bricks, crunching his jaw and blasting his teeth out. I was rushing off thoughts of torturing him and getting him to a state where he'll never be the same again. I din't tell them lot what I was fantasising about, 'cause I don't really know if other people think like that. I'm not sure, but there must be others out there that think fucked-up things to do to people.

'What you thinking?' Boo Boo asked, as I started skinning up again. I was day-dreaming that I had sliced Robert Henley's fingers open and was pouring salt on the cuts, but I replied, looking at her cute face and bright blue eyes, 'Just thinking of my mum.'

'What about her?' I had a feeling Boo Boo Girl was trying to distract herself from whatever hundred-mile-per-hour thoughts were zipping through her brain. I din't wanna lie, and I din't wanna put her on more of a downer, so we spoke about our parents for a while and I tried to keep us on mums so we din't mention her dad.

'I can't believe she kicked me out,' I said, on about my mum kicking me out the house when I turned sixteen for summat I din't do. By the time I was sat there with Boo, as Valerie and Martin tracked that bastard down, I'd not spoken to my mother for over a year. I wanted to, I just got stubborn. My mum's stubborn, too, so that din't help. I even walked past her in the street without saying hello. I suppose I wanted to punish her for punishing me.

'But if she wun't have booted me out,' I told Boo

Boo, 'I'd never have met you!'

Boo smiled gently. 'And them two and the lads.'

I smiled back. 'Exactly, we're getting on with it aren't we mate?'

We leaned over to kiss each other on the lips, not a romantic kiss, just a kiss between good mates. Me, Boo Boo and Valerie were always like that.

I told her, 'I love you, you know that don't you?'

Boo Boo Girl goes, 'Of course, and I love you too.'

Valerie and Martin started making loads of noise in the phone box, jumping around and shouting. I clicked open the passenger door and poked my head out.

'What's 'appened?' I yelled. They couldn't hear me and came out waving the pieces of paper, punching the air, high-fiving and laughing.

Valerie screamed. 'We've fucking found 'im, man!'

I was like, 'Wow,' looking at Boo, who looked shocked with her eyebrows raised.

We drove away excited, with Martin going over what happened on the phone.

He was like, 'So this woman answers and she's like, "Good morning, the Moat House", and I'm trying to sound all posh and I goes, "Yes, hello, I am trying to locate my uncle, I wondered if he is still staying there?", and she asks, "What's his name please?", and I'm like "Robert Henley," and she goes, "One moment, please," and then she comes back and goes, "Yes, your uncle is still with us would you like me to put you through to his room?", and I'm like, "Yes please," but I put it down. I can't believe we found him: at the fuckin' Moat House!'

The Moat House was across the Forest Recreation Ground from the hostel; we even drove past it a couple of times the day before. He was close to us all along.

We felt proud of ourselves. A bunch of nobodies locating a rapist, tracking him down, that's what it was. I learnt that day that you can get jobs done if you go out and get on with it.

Sat in the car, buzzing at finding him, I was secretly not wanting them lot to be involved; not because they din't deserve it, they were Boo Boo's friends as much as me, but because it had been my idea, my fantasy, and my trudging up and down West Bridgford for three or four days. I din't come up with the ringing 'round all the hotels but I could have done, with a few more days thinking, especially as Boo Boo probably would have told me about where he was anyway.

I was jealous in a stupid way, 'cause Valerie and Martin suddenly started taking over. The plan was how they saw, the way they wanted it. Mainly it was their age and the fact that they spent longer than me in the phone box ringing up. I couldn't knock them for that, I just din't rate their plan.

8 On the Move

We waited all day Monday, parked up in Martin's Renault, but we din't see Henley. Martin said not to smoke or drink, so we could concentrate, but we did smoke a bit. Back then we smoked just about all the time.

It's tricky to remember, I mean, the exact details of how it happened. I can't remember how long we staked out the car park, whether it was two days or four, and facts like that. It's become blurred, all the billy and draw I've taken has fucked with my memory. There were definitely people in the car park shouting, 'Leave 'im alone!' as we snatched his keys and rushed him into the car. We were mainly relying on Martin, 'cause me and Valerie couldn't do it on our own, that's why it was hot, because Robert Henley was quite strong for a little guy who looked like he din't have strength.

Henley was like, 'Get off me! What do you think you're doing?'

Valerie roared at him, 'Shut ya fuckin mouth ya fuckin' nonce!' She started punching him in his face and chest.

We couldn't get him to the Renault, so Martin was like, 'In his car, in his car!' We shoved Henley into the boot of his Rover.

An old man and woman, sat in a red Skoda, parked right near us, watched with their mouths open. It felt surreal and it must have looked it.

Robert Henley was wailing and screaming for help as he hit the boot. Martin told Valerie to drive as she jumped in and I dived onto the back seat, sweating and looking around for anyone tryna be a hero. Valerie couldn't drive too tough, but she sped out of that car-park rapid, and still someone was shouting at us as we drove off. Martin had fucked off in his car with Boo Boo to try and meet up with us later.

My heart was vibrating my whole chest, and I din't wanna say how scared I was because Valerie was swearing loads, going, 'Fuckinell, fuckinell!' She even stalled the engine a couple of times on the way out of Nottingham.

'We should have tied him up,' I said. Valerie din't reply.

I was looking out for the police, who I expected to be blue-lighting us at any moment, while Valerie did a decent job of getting us off the main roads and into the countryside without crashing.

We had no idea what happened to Boo Boo Girl and Martin, thinking they were behind us by a few minutes, catching up.

We pulled into one of those lonely lanes near Clumber Park, like a farmer's lane that goes on for miles. It was getting dark. We opened the boot and he was still going on, trying to get out, so we pushed him back in and Valerie punched him and bust his lip. He looked a pathetic mess in his bloodied white shirt and blue trousers.

'Stop fucking shouting!' I said and snapped my fist against his cheek. The stinging contact made my knuckles burn, but I enjoyed it.

Valerie screamed, 'Give us ya wallet!' She cracked Henley over and over in his ribs and he actually began to cry.

Each time he tried to get out, we pushed him back and Valerie kept whacking him. I was getting excited. We got the wallet from him after Valerie had smacked him so many times in his stomach he had blood and tears and sweat dripping off his chin. I kicked him in the eye, which brought it up red and puffy. He was shouting for help. We kept hurting him. He had a blue tool-box in his boot and Valerie bounced that off his head a few times and smashed it on his feet, 'cause we dashed his shoes away. We gave him a right going-over.

I pulled out Dogknife from my trainer and gripped the handle 'till my knuckles were white.

Valerie was like, 'What the fuck are ya doin'?'

Robert Henley's face and was nothing but blood and fear.

9 Power

Martin and Boo Boo Girl were arrested in the Renault more or less as soon as they left the hotel car park, which was sixty seconds after me and Valerie skidded away with Robert Henley in the boot.

A hotel worker had seen us rushing him and ran back inside the hotel to ring the police. The witness gave the police a description of Martin's Renault because they saw him sprint back to it as me and Valerie got in the Rover. Obviously we din't know about that until we got back to the hostel the next afternoon - 'cause we went to stay at Valerie's mate's in Clifton after we left Henley - and the staff told us they'd been arrested and asked us if we knew anything. We played dumb, pretending we had no clue what the fuck they were talking about. Boo Boo's mum came to the hostel to ask me what happened and I lied to her as well.

The lads were shocked that Boo Boo had been done for assault and aggravated theft. Only Valerie and me knew those charges din't make any sense because it was us that drove off in the car with Robert Henley in the boot. When we were rushing him Boo Boo stayed in Martin's car.

Police arrest people on trumped up charges until they can figure out who did what and which charge might stick and which ones are bang-to-rights. Me and Valerie were more worried about Martin and his car being involved, and we din't know what trouble he was going to get in for it. We started getting rid of the evidence, like our blood stained tops and bandanas, and we cleaned ourselves up as best we could.

Martin and Boo Boo were released later that night after we'd got back, and we found out that they'd been charged with conspiracy to kidnap because the police had linked them to the car park, and Robert Henley who was found by a farmer near to where we left him. Martin told the police that he had dropped off some of his mates at the hotel and left. He refused to name us, so the police din't have real evidence on him. Boo Boo said she was in Martin's car just to hang out. Police said that was a coincidence being that Henley had been acquitted of raping her. Boo Boo ignored that, but said the other people in the car who got out at the hotel were girls, but she was too scared to name them. The coppers weren't daft though and they were sniffing around the hostel the day after those two were released, when we were all in and watching them search. They even had a warrant, looking all over the place, in all the rooms, through everyone's stuff, all their drawers and their clothes and pockets and purses. They asked us all questions, all the residents. The police were trying to find out who hung around with Boo Boo Girl and Martin.

Not all the boys and girls that live in gritty inner-city hostels are street-wise, which is what you might think, so loads of residents gave statements about who was dossing with Boo Boo. In a way it wasn't their fault, a lot of people are scared of authority, especially the police who can take away your freedom in a flash, but if they'd shut their faces then maybe the petty officers wouldn't have returned with the CID. They came at six in the morning, with new warrants to go through all my stuff and turn mine and Valerie's rooms upside down.

Valerie was going mad, swearing, 'Who the fuck do you think you are?' She was first to get nicked, mainly 'cause she was kicking off and being cheeky. I fucked up though, massively. Two objects were found linking me directly to the attack: Dogknife, which still had microscopic bits of blood on it, wrapped in a towel down the back of my radiator, and Robert Henley's credit card, stashed under my carpet.

I was fucked, but I still tried to blag it. I said they weren't mine and I din't put 'em there but a friend did, and I can't name the friend because I'm not a grass.

I kept telling them they couldn't prove I put them there, yet all they needed to convince a jury was to say I probably did, and I'd get convicted. If they wouldn't have found the card and Dogknife they would have had nothing to link me to the attack. My trainers din't have blood on them, so that link was circumstantial, or whatever ya call it.

I'd had Dogknife for eight years and there was no way I could get rid of it. Dogknife was part of my everyday existence. I should have chucked the credit card, but I liked the new look and shine it had. I read in true-crime magazines that some criminals liked to keep trophies, like symbols and objects, to remind them of what they'd done. I had a Robert Henley trophy. I couldn't stop thinking about what I'd done, and looking at the new card made it feel like revenge was proper. I felt dangerous, in a good way. I stabbed him, and he's never going to forget me or the look in my eyes when I stuck Dogknife into him. My eyes would have been bulging with adrenalin and excitement.

Valerie was shocked and going, 'Oh my god! You fucking stabbed him!' I was what-d'ya-call-it? Frenzied. I was frenzied, or hypnotised, and probably would have stabbed Valerie if she tried to stop me, especially since the time she shamed me when she said I couldn't walk the beat.

I wasn't even thinking of that when I was jukking Henley though, I was just focusing on where to stab him so it wun't kill him. I din't want him to die, I wanted him to stay alive and see the scars everyday in the mirror, so he would be reminded of what he did to Boo Boo Girl. If he wouldn't have raped my mate, I wouldn't have stabbed him. That's the whole point, it's like a cycle. A cycle of violence.

The evidence they had on me was the credit card,

Dogknife, and statements from idiots in the hostel saying I was best mates with Martin, Boo Boo, and Valerie. They had descriptions from Henley of girls attacking him and one of the girls stabbing him. They had my trainers as well, which din't help. I din't think to go on the run, I thought we wun't get caught for a start, but I could've stayed at a school-mate's house for a bit. I would have got kicked out the hostel and the police would have caught up with me eventually, I suppose, seeing as I would have carried on working the beat and coppers would have stopped me on the street.

I wasn't really thinking of that though, I was going over and over the stabbing.

I'd stabbed him, I felt powerful, different to before, like special. Even Valerie was shocked and that's saying summat.

10 No Comment

I1A - Page 1 Police Copy UNR - 22210
Police Interview Stephanie Walters Ref: A09/03/43777
DC SWINTON. PC WILLIAMS. JANSONS PARTNERS
SOLICITORS. 23/07/99
00:00 Formal introductions and caution
02:13
DCS: Stephanie, at six forty this morning you were arrested by officer Williams and one of his colleagues, on suspicion of the attempted murder of Robert Henley in the early evening of Wednesday the twentieth of July, which was Wednesday this week... Mister Henley was stabbed twice in the hand, once in the face, once in the neck, and once in his upper right leg... Do you want to tell us what you know about this attack?
02:33
SW: No comment.
DCS: This is your opportunity to tell us about what happened.
02:39
SW: No comment.
DCS: Mister Henley received over one-hundred stitches for his wounds and is in a state of shock and considerable pain... Do you want to tell us why you attacked him?
SW: No comment.
02:52
DCS: Who else attacked him?
SW: No comment.
02:55
DCS: Did Martin Howard, who lives in your hostel, did he take part?
SW: No comment.
03:00

DCS: But you are friends with Martin Howard?

SW: No comment.

03:04

DCS: We've got a statement made by Martin Howard, which he gave to us on the same evening, Wednesday evening just past, after he was arrested on suspicion of aggravated vehicle taking and assault... That's what he was arrested for okay... In this statement he says he and you are good mates and that you were... In his car minutes before he was arrested.

I1A - Page 2 Police Copy UNR - 22210

Police interview Stephanie Walters Ref: A09/03/43777

DC SWINTON. PC WILLIAMS. JANSONS PARTNERS SOLICITORS. 23/07/99

(continued)

DCS: Is that true?

SW: No comment.

03:33

DCS: Okay... I'm going to read Robert Henley's first statement, I'm going to read some of it and I'd like you to listen very carefully... In the beginning section he states who he is and where he lives and he also describes himself and the car he owns... I'm going to read from this section... 'I came out of the hotel's rear entrance and proceeded across the car-park towards my car, which was parked close to a number of other cars of other residents. The visibility was good, it was very light outside and still warm, I was around ten feet from my car and I had the keys in my right hand, I depressed the central locking button on my key ring, then I was aware of movement, or the sound of walking behind me, I could hear the rustling of clothing, the sound of jeans and tracksuits, that sort of sound. I turned to see who it could be, and was startled to see three people really close to me, coming towards me, I'd say they were two to three feet away when I turned around to look at them. I would describe them as follows: the tallest was a male with black hair that was frizzy and looked quite greasy, I shall refer to him as Attacker One. Attacker One was about six foot one and skinny, I could tell he was skinny because he had a black sleeveless t-shirt on and his arms were thin. He had a pair of scruffy blue jeans with holes in the knees, I remember these details because he was the first attacker I saw after I turned around he had a...

I1A - Page 3 Police Copy UNR - 22210

Police interview Stephanie Walters Ref: A09/03/43777

DC SWINTON. PC WILLIAMS. JANSONS PARTNERS SOLICITORS. 23/07/99

(continued)

04:45

...Black bandana with white shapes on it over his face below the eyes, I don't recall what colour eyes he had. He wore black footwear but I don't remember if they were shoes or trainers, but they were all black, he did not appear to be holding anything in his hands. Attacker Two I would describe as a female, around five foot nine, I could tell she was female straight away as I could see the shape of her breasts through the top she wore, it was a black hooded jumper, she had on a blue baseball cap with the black hood pulled over it, on the front of the cap the word Nike, the sports manufacturer, the writing was white. Attacker Two had on shiny tracksuit trousers that were black and she had black footwear too, she also wore a black bandana over her lower face, under her eyes. Attacker Three was also a female but smaller than Attacker Two, I'd say between five foot seven and five foot eight, and also wearing a black hooded sports top with the hood pulled over her head and around her face. The rest of her face was covered with a black bandana the same as Attacker One and Two. I could tell Attacker Three was a girl as her breasts were also protruding through her clothes, she had black jeans and black trainers with three white stripes down their side, the name Adidas on them, the trainer company. At that point I became scared, as they came closer I asked them what they wanted and Attacker One, the male, punched me hard in the face, hitting me in my right cheek and he told me to move and they all began grabbing me and forcing me towards my car. They pulled me to the boot of the car, they were all hitting me as I recall, but it was hard to say which attacker exactly hit me and when, I felt pain in my back and face and was very scared, I do not know why they were attacking me like that, all I could think of was to try and get away from them. I started shouting for help but that only made them angrier and caused them to hit me more, there seemed to be no-one around to help and I was getting sore and running out of breath. I'm not totally certain which attacker opened my car's boot, but one of them did and then they shoved me in violently. They twisted my arms until they felt like they were going to break, and they pushed on them to get me into the boot of my car. I was still very frightened by it all, they locked me in the boot and then I was very scared for my safety.'

PAGE 66

I1A - Page 4 Police Copy UNR - 22210

Police interview Stephanie Walters Ref: A09/03/43777

DC SWINTON. PC WILLIAMS. JANSONS PARTNERS SOLICITORS. 23/07/99

(continued)

06:48

DCS; Is that you, Attacker Three?

SW: No comment.

DCS: I think that it is; we think that it is, that it is you.

SW: No comment.

PCW: Stephanie, this is your chance to put your side across to us and explain your involvement.

07:01

SW: No comment.

DCS: The trainers you were wearing when you were arrested... Will you describe them for us?

07:06

SW: No comment.

DCS: How long have you had them for?

SW: No comment.

07:10

DCS: A month?

SW: No comment.

07:12

DCS: A week?

SW: No comment.

07:14

DCS: For the tape, Stephanie was wearing black and white Adidas trainers, with white stripes down each side and the words Adidas on them. That's interesting, don't you think?

SW: No comment.

07:24

DCS: We'll be conducting further tests on the trainers fairly soonish, that's right they've been sent, get ready, yeah.

PSW: Yeah, sure, Gary should have done that... (inaudible)

DCS: Would you say you were around five foot seven inches tall?

SW: No comment.

07:35

DCS: But you are that height aren't you, because my colleagues measured you in the custody suite?

SW: No comment.

07:39

DCS: Going back to Mister Henley's statement, I want you to listen to the following: 'I thought they were going to crash the car, the reason I thought that is because of the way the car was being driven.

I1A - Page 5 Police Copy UNR - 22210

Police interview Stephanie Walters Ref: A09/03/43777

DC SWINTON. PC WILLIAMS. JANSONS PARTNERS SOLICITORS. 23/07/99

(continued)

DCS: It was very erratic and it made me think they din't know how to drive, I was scared they were going to crash whilst I was in the boot.' Is that you, the person driving dangerously?

SW: No comment.

07:59
DCS: Can you tell us who was driving?
SW: No comment.
08:01
DCS: Do you drive?
SW: No comment.
08:03
PCW: Can any of your mates drive?
SW: No comment.
08:06
DCS: Returning now to the statement... Mister Henley states: 'I still had my watch on, and it has a light on it, so I could tell the time, and it was eight-fifteen pm and I estimate I had been attacked and forced into the boot around ten to fifteen minutes before. I had no clue where they had taken me, and I was becoming more and more panicky. I was screaming for help and banging on the inside of the car with my fists, it was eight-thirty pm when the car stopped and they switched the engine off, I had no idea where they had taken me, I heard the sound of the boot opening and then the doors opening and then they came to the boot and lifted the hood. They no longer had the bandanas over their faces except they were still round their necks, I could see they were clearly girls definitely. Attacker Two, who was still wearing the Nike cap, looked gaunt and pale with a thin face and an angry look in her eyes. She looked menacing. Attacker Three still had the hood up over her head, I would describe her face as slightly round, and she looked young and scared. I would also describe Attacker Two's eyes as brown, and Attacker Three's eyes as hazel or greeny-blue. I then tried to climb from the boot but they carried on hitting me, Attacker Two started the violence against me.'
DCS: Stop the time for - (inaudible).

11 Juk

People treated me different, giving me drags on spliffs, or setting me fags or a liquor, just because they were wary or bummy. I noticed that lads backed off too, stopped hassling me for shines and cash, and I got invited to parties they were going to. I was getting a reputation because of stabbing Henley. I din't think about it until Sharon mentioned it, then I realised people were wary of me, as if I would go 'round slashing 'em up for no reason.

Sharon was a goodie-goodie, din't do drugs or smoke fags or spliffs, but she was most people's friend. She went to college and had a part-time job, I suppose she was good looking, but she never had a boyfriend or one-off that I new of. Sharon was normal on the outside, I think she was fucked up inside though, like the rest of us in that place. She wan't a snob or ote. She had bloke hair, short and dykey looking. I'm not saying she was a lesbian, but she dressed like a boy dyke, with trousers and shirts, so she might have been. I don't care.

About a week or two after I got charged I was stood in the kitchen area, which was next to the sitting room where we watched films, and it was what they call open plan or whatever, with the kitchen next to it so you can still watch television and chat to people when you're cooking. I was making a cup of coffee; I loved coffee, with loads of sugar. Sharon came in and started making cheese-on-toast, getting out the bread and a small plate and the grater and cheese and all that. I stood watching Sharon, not saying note - just clocking her. I din't fancy her, I like watching people doing everyday bits-and-bobs. Sharon wouldn't have been my type any road, too chubby for me. Girls in shirts and trousers don't get me going.

Sharon wanted to have her penny's worth. 'I heard about what ya did, Stephanie.'

Sharon din't look at me. She was stood across from me, grating the lump of cheddar. I was waiting for the kettle to boil.

Even though it was summer I was wearing an Adidas tracksuit, a pair of classic three stripes, blue with white stripes, and a pair of women's black leather driving gloves. I couldn't even drive then, but I liked the feel and look of them. Nowadays you see kids walking 'round with golf gloves, driving gloves, and baseball gloves and that, but back in the day only rude-girls wore gloves like leathers, especially in summer. I'm not saying I was a rude-girl or anything, but I wasn't an angel, that's for sure. I liked the look, I could pull it off.

Sharon carried on, 'Is that what ya gonna do with ya life then, stab people?'

'He deserved it,' I said, smiling.

'Nobody deserves to be stabbed.'

Sharon was full of herself, as if she knew what it was all about. I din't reckon she was a snob when it came to living in a trampy hostel in the dodgy part of a rough city, but she had an opinion on most subjects. Stood there in her fucking orange and whatever checked shirt, telling me like she knows me. Sharon hadn't been in the hostel long enough to know the score, so I told her.

'If ya must know, he raped Boo Boo Girl and got off with it,' I turned to deal with my drink, 'so he fucking deserved it as far as I'm concerned.'

'Oh, I din't know that.'

I stirred the water into the mixture in my cup and goes, 'That's why I did it, revenge.' I tapped the spoon on the side of the cup when I said revenge, like ding-ding, *revenge*.

'You could have taken it too far, he could have been killed.'

'So?'

'Is that what you wanna be, a murderer?' I reckon she loved the sound of her own voice and wan't really thinking about what she was saying. How could another girl not want a rapist to get done over? Fuck that. Sharon was clever, read books and went to protests about people's rights; rights to be gay, rights to smoke weed, rights to this and the next thing. It din't mean she was right all the time.

'Of course I don't.'

'But you think stabbing people is okay?'

'Don't worry about me,' I said, 'I ain't gonna be no murderer. And anyway, it was revenge.'

I din't want to talk to her.

Sharon went, 'People will have to watch themselves around you now then, is that how it's going to be?'

I took a sip of coffee.

'Not at all,' I said, 'if people don't mess with me then I won't bring trouble to them.'

'Just be careful, that's all I'm saying.'

I went, 'Whatever,' and walked off to sit down.

Sharon stuck her cheese-on-toast on a plate and fucked off.

I was still working the beat and getting on with it, but I was worried about my charges. I din't wanna go to prison. No way. At attendance centre for the robberies before, the older girls used to swap stories about what jails they'd been in and who they knew. They told us stories of girls shitting in the food in the kitchens, actually shitting in it. Human shit, in ya fucking food. Horrible. Then they told us about the strip-searches, being naked all the time in front of women screws, checking to see if you've got weapons or drugs. Their stories scared me.

When I lay on my bed after I'd done a couple of punters, smoking a zoot or twiddling my thumbs, I had little panic attacks wondering how I would survive prison if I got found guilty. The walls would wobble a bit, that's what it was like, and I'd shut my eyes to make the feeling go away, my heart pumping more than usual and I'd be suddenly sweating loads. Proper panic attacks. I pretended to not be bothered when friends or staff asked about the case.

I'd be like, 'I'm getting a not-guilty, definitely!'

Even if they were asking, 'What about the knife they found in your room?'

I'd say summat like, 'They can't prove it's mine just because they found it in my room!'

I was in wotcha-call-it? Denial. I was in denial that I was bang to rights and gonna get a guilty. What I din't know when I was bigging myself up to Sharon in the kitchen was that I had one more month of freedom left until I was banged up on remand. My life changed like never before, even moving out of home, dissing school or working the beat combined couldn't compare to being locked up.

The Bolsover Hotel
Derbyshire
September 15th 1999
Dear Barbara,

I'd like to say thank you for your last letter and the photo of the boys, which now sits pride of place atop the hotel rooms' TV set! To be frank, there's little else in this room, you know me - I don't require large comforts.

Well the trial starts soon but only two of them will be there as the man that helped them was dealt with in the magistrate's court two weeks ago. He received a community sentence order totaling two hundred hours and a sentence of ten months, suspended for a year. Personally I'm not happy at the Judge's decision, as I feel a prison sentence would deter him from ever doing crime again. Still, the matter is nearly at an end.

My scars are healing well. They still look angry and are sore to touch, but they've closed up properly and there's no infection left, so that's great for my health.

Enough of me; how are you? How are the boys? I miss them - and you, obviously - and can't wait to see them next weekend, as long as that agreement still stands? Is it still ok? I've been looking forward to it.

Tell them I send my love, as usual, and I'll see them very soon.
Goodbye for now Barb', all my love and thoughts,
Rob.

PS. The cheque is for bills, with more to follow.

12 Remand

The trial at Nottingham Crown Court started after months of paperwork was dealt with by magistrates 'round the corner.

Statements had been gathered from all over the place; a couple in the hotel car park that watched us attacking Henley and putting him in the boot; passengers sat in cars and workers looking out of hotel windows; two young girls on bikes at traffic lights who went home and told their parents to ring the police because they heard a man screaming from a car boot and they remembered the car reg' number.

Waterloo residents gave statements saying me and Valerie and Boo Boo were best-mates and hung around all the time. The police kind of knew that from Boo Boo's case because we were there for her every time she dealt with the police liaison people, whatever they're called.

There was all sorts of evidence; photographs of Henley's cuts, bruises and slashes; Dogknife; my trainers; Valerie's hair from the driver's seat; statements from Henley about what happened to him and even one about how messed up in the head he was after it had finished. Henley said he might have to have plastic surgery, which a doctor backed up in another statement.

There was forensic evidence; how much force was used against him; type of blade used; blood types, blood stains and other forensic shit. Photographs of Henley all battered up, inside the car, all the stains in the boot, the damage to the car, CCTV of the car driving out of town, witnesses who saw the car, watched the car and heard sounds from the boot. Those statements came from people who had seen the police advert on the side of the road about an incident and grassed up what they knew.

Valerie and me already knew which evidence was going to be used against us, but you only get the real vibe when it's being read out loud in court. We both looked at each other nervous as ote and we din't dare look at the jury.

Valerie ended up saying, 'Well, he fucking raped Boo Boo Girl so he deserved what he got, why should he walk 'round Notts' scott free?' Valerie was crying and I'd never seen her break down like that, falling to bits in the stand.

When it was my turn I denied it all the way. It was obvious it was me that stabbed him, but I wan't just gonna sit there and admit it. Fuck that.

A member of staff from the hostel helped the court by making a statement saying I carried a knife everywhere I went. The prosecution bloke, who had a daft wig on, wore a posh suit and had a big moustache, asked me why I had Dogknife. He was talking all posh like, 'For what purpose did the knife intend to serve?'

I told him straight, 'It's for in case I have to fight a dog, so I don't get chewed up or killed.'

He said that seemed like odd behaviour.

'You can think what you want,' I told him.

It took the jury two hours to find us guilty on all the charges, and my mouth went dry and I was dead nervous when they read out the verdict. Valerie got guilty on kidnap, TWOC, robbery and ABH; I got guilty on kidnap, robbery and GBH.

None of Valerie's family was in court and she just looked down at the floor. My mum was there and she started crying when they said we were guilty. For some daft reason I was smiling at my mum. All the court workers, the secretaries, the public waiting for other cases to start, the clerks and the other bods mooching about, all looked over at us with no expressions on their faces.

I felt like a ghost, like it wasn't real life or I was in a mad dream.

The prosecution told the Judge he thought we'd do

a runner if we got bail before sentencing, so he recommended that we get remanded there and then. The Judge believed him and he remanded us for sentencing six weeks later. That was it - jail.

My mum screamed at the Judge, 'They're just girls!'

The security took us away and down the long, smelly steps to the court cells. They din't place me in a cell straight away because my mum wanted to visit me in the glass-screened visit booths. I waited near the court cells reception, stood next to a fat female screw, a Group 4 guard, waiting for my mum to take her seat in the visits section. I sat on one side of the glass and my mum on the other.

Mum's worry, that's what they do. My mum is the same as the rest of them, always worrying about me and what I'm up to. There were times in my life when she din't worry enough, so we went without, but I know life's been a struggle for her in its own way. She was pregnant with my older sister, Jade, when she was fifteen and had her when she was sixteen, then preggers with me when she was seventeen, and had me when she was eighteen, and was pregnant again with Sebella at nineteen and had her at twenty. If that ain't pressure on a girl, then I don't know what is. My mum was also a heroin addict for ten years, but I don't know when she started. She tooted it, when you hold a lighter under some foil with brown on it and the fumes rise up and you suck them down as much as you can to get monged, using a pipe of rolled up foil. They call it tooting or booting and it's famous as *chasing-the-dragon*.

I remember days when we did go without and that meant we were poor and I was ashamed. I never wanted my friends to come around to the house or stay the night, because they'd see the dirty kitchen floor and greasy cooker, the smelly toilet and bathroom, our dirty beds and mattresses, manky pillows, cheap toys and badly made, low-priced clothes. I din't want my friends to know I was a tramp.

My best mates had houses that were three times the

size of any of the shit holes I've lived in; their parents had proper jobs and could afford to give my mates everything they needed, and most of what they wanted as well. They weren't snobs or ote, at least not to my face; they had more stable upbringings is all. I wanted what they had: nice food in the fridge all the time, money when I needed it, bus fares, pocket money, all that shit. I wan't dead jealous or ote, they were my mates before they knew I was poor and even now I can sit down with a couple of them and have a laugh and get on. One thing I never did was steal from their houses - not even a quid on the side or a chocolate bar from the tin. When I was seven or eight and living in The Meadows, some of my friends had gadgets and toys and stuff like fold-in-half sunglasses, and I would nick them and keep them for myself because I din't know any better until I was older, with my older mates, the ones I met at comprehensive school, and who lived out of The Meadows in nice areas like Mapperly and Sherwood. Their houses were big and they had money and better jobs, but I couldn't steal off them. I din't want to.

Their life showed me mine could be different, I could reach a place in life when I would have what they took for granted. Those mates, like Rachel Robbins and Catherine Searson, treated me like an equal, so I din't give a shit if they were better off then me. My mum made an effort when Rachel or Catherine came round to doss after school to listen to tunes or have a joke and read mags'. She'd hoover up and wash the pots, she din't swear or smoke weed and spoke a bit posher. That's what I wanted her to do. I wanted to pretend I was living like them and for them to believe I was. I would have died if they had known how poor and trampy we really were.

Now it's daft, but then it was serious because my mates were the best thing I had going in my life and my friendship with them made me escape the stress, arguing and fighting at home. If I stayed over at one of their houses, in a clean, spare bed with fresh sheets and bed covers, even borrowing a brand new tooth brush and wearing some clean jimjams, my poor life din't exist because I was one of them. I even pretended once that I was their sister and that my family and home life wasn't real. That's the way your imagination works when ya poor.

People think you can't be poor in this country, but you can. All you need are the wrong set of circumstances. It's not going to be like places in the world where there's no running water or electric, living in a shack in the middle of a boiling hot country in Africa. Being poor in England will still mess up your health and mental state. There's plenty of kids in this country going without, not just 'cause their mum is a junky or their dad is in jail, it's 'cause money is always involved - either there's not enough or what they do have goes on the wrong things.

The look on my mum's face, when I sat down opposite her in the glass-screened visit booth, was nothing more than straightforward upset. I could tell she'd been crying hard before she came in, her eyes were red raw where she'd been rubbing tears away stressing about me being in trouble. I was nervous about going to a young offender's institute, after all the horror stories I'd heard that were still fresh in my head, but I was talking loads and acting all cool, like I din't give two shits. Obviously my mum could see through my mask, and her pain was probably to do with the fact that in my heart of hearts I was gutted and not looking forward to becoming a prisoner. I looked at my mum as she was trying not to cry and I was like, 'Don't worry about me ma, I'm a survivor, I'm going to be alright and Valerie will be with me and we'll get on with it, d' y' get me?'

I was putting on a brave face. My mum left crying into tissues and the first shock I got after she went was when one of the Group 4 screws told me Valerie was going to a different prison from me.

I frowned.

'Ow come?'

'The police told us that she's had trouble with a girl at Glen Dale, where you're going.'

'Where's she going then?' I couldn't remember Val having beef with anyone in Glen Dale.

'A women's prison.'

With desperation in my voice I cried, 'But she's a teenager like me!'

'They've got a YP wing there, so that's where we're sending her.'

'Thanks,' I said glumly. The massive metal door on the smelly holding cell slammed shut. I sat there and tears starting welling up. I was going to jail. Valerie was not going with me. Mum was heart-broken.

The walls were vibrating in on me. I pressed the emergency button. A buzzing sound kicked in and I heard a man's voice outside my door saying, 'I've got it.'

A second later the wooden flap covering the observation window lifted up and there was a Group 4 screw stood there.

'What's up?'

'Can I please see a doctor or a nurse or someone because I don't feel good, I feel panicky.' My eyes were pleading.

'Look,' he softened his tone and leaned against the inside of the cell doorway, 'the nurse has gone for the day. I don't usually do this, but you can have the door open until your bus comes for Glen Dale, okay?'

'Thank you,' I said.

It would be two whole years until someone in authority treated me like a human being again.

13 My Bird

You could read a hundred books about going inside prison for the first time, about getting loaded onto the sweatbox security bus with tinted windows that make the sky look weird; you can see out, but no-one can see in; a tight little space to sit during the journey.

Once you arrive it's always the same set up: big walls, fences with barbed wire, screws with keys on chains, CCTV, and big gates and doors. The reception area where they strip you, search you and give you a toothbrush, a cup, a bowl, a knife, fork, and spoon - all plastic shit - toothpaste and some pieces of paper with rules and regulations written all over them. They also give you your prison number and take your photo. Then they tell you what wing you're going on and you wait until everyone else who came in with you has been, wotcha-call-it? Processed. After all the other girls have been processed, you go to your new home.

Two vibes that I picked up on straight away was the smell of the place and the massive feelings of loneliness.

The pong was like the one you get in hospitals because the whole area has to be detergent cleaned everyday, but it was also mixed with summat else, like the grim smell of a place that doesn't get much sunlight or fresh air through windows. It's a smell you don't forget, believe me.

The loneliness: you feel it as soon as you're stood waiting to be celled – wearing washed, but crap fitting prison tracksuits - desperate for company. Even when a screw was asking me what religion I was and whether I had suicidal thoughts or special food requirements, I wanted to be near another person, to stay talking to him, not be on my todd in a locked room. The screw probably din't give a shit about me, but it was good to be with another being that's breathing and living. It's like if you're sat at home watching a horror film and you're shitting yourself, but you've got a dog or cat with you so it's alright.

I tried to take no notice of the five or six other girls that were waiting to get taken to a cell. They seemed older than me; even if they weren't, I felt like the youngest. One of them only had one arm and all the others, who all looked like smack-heads because they had greasy hair and were scabby and skinny and sniffing up snot all the while, were asking about it and touching the stump. I just sat staring at the floor trying to have a serious face on me. Valerie told me you've got to look mean and then people ain't in a rush to fuck with you. I sat there looking moody, in a room like a doctor's waiting area, with ten shitty chairs welded to the floor and two CCTV cameras watching us.

After an hour or more of waiting, a red-faced screw with a rough Scouse accent, angry eyes and tense fists, came into the room.

'Right then, scum-bags, lets go!'

We followed the mardy screw, who one of the other girls called 'Mister S.', along a series of corridors, which were dark and smelly. We rushed to keep up with Mister S. and his clip-clop steps and after three or four minutes of skipping behind we stopped at a shut set of thick metal gates that were in front of two heavy wooden doors. The screw read quickly from a clip-board and some of the girls reacted rapidly, as if they were expecting to be smacked if they din't move fast enough. Unlocking the gates and doors he ushered them onto the wing. The Scouse screw said, 'Off you go, losers,' and another screw waiting for them showed them the room to sit in and shut the doors on us.

Mister S. glared at the rest of us.

'You idiots, follow me.'

We marched down more corridors and then stopped at another set of gates in front of more locked, heavy wooden doors. There was me, the one-armed girl, and a mix-raced girl with Indian ink tattoos on her arms and neck.

In his gruff voice, Mister S. goes, 'Welcome to Unit 14,' for some reason he turned to me and grinned like a nutter, 'or Beirut, as it's often called'.

He came onto the wing with us because that's where he worked full-time.

The noise of fifty or more girls out on association, when they can ring home and play pool and games of cards or whatever, hit me straight away. They had table-tennis and table-football, too. The association area was like the size of a tennis court. A few voices called out to the mixed-race girl, who answered to 'Shanty', not her real name, who waved back and shouted, 'Yeah, safe rude-girl, good to see ya!' She walked into the space and up to a small crowd of girls around a pool table. The screws din't care that Shanty was doing her own thing.

I din't want to stare at anyone so I turned to watch the Scouse officer chatting to a few more screws in a tiny office, with windows all around it, next to where we came in. The windows of the office let them see what was going on in the entire association space. There and then I couldn't see any cells.

We were told to go in the office and a different officer told us to grab some blankets and sheets from a little cupboard. We followed him through the association room to a large door that led to the corridors, what they call landings. We went up the stairs inside until we got to the top, or the three's landing, and we walked to cell thirteen.

'Walters and Harris in here.' We shuffled into the cell and the musty air was rank with the smell of cheesy feet and sweat.

'You might wanna open the window to let some air in,' said the screw, 'and don't press the emergency bell unless one of you's dying or you'll be in trouble'.

'No problem boss,' said Harris, the girl with one arm.

The screw locked us in and that was it: I was in jail proper and I was seventeen years old.

It was claustrophobic like a bastard, the walls were moving in and it was hard to breathe, with panic attacks that lasted a few minutes each time. I din't enjoy the feeling of being trapped. The cell was small, the size of a tiny kitchen. There was a metal toilet to the right with a metal sink on the wall next to it. In front of me were the ends of two bunk beds that went to the back wall, which had a barred window on, and under the window were two metal chunks coming out of the wall for chairs. There was a small bin, a toilet roll holder, a light switch for the strip light on the ceiling, and the emergency bell. Just like the hostel, where people din't give a shit about the floors and that, there were stains all over and graffiti on the walls and door. The cell needed a good clean out, that's for sure. The view from the window was simple: fences, bland prison buildings, plenty of barbed wire and large CCTV cameras dotted here and there. About a mile away in the distance I could make out a few trees and other buildings, probably houses and shops. That was it. I was shut off from the outside world. I din't know when I was going to be able to see it again properly. I was on edge, I din't want no trouble and I was panicky about the claustrophobia, and I was shocked about being in jail, locked away with other criminals, but I wan't depressed there and then. The sadness came later when I got my sentence.

There's no way it was an adventure, I obviously would've rather been free, so I was saying to myself, 'Right, lets see what happens now, what life's gonna throw at me.' I wan't going to take no shit from the other girls, that's for sure.

Valerie said to kick off straight away if somebody started and never back down if some bitch was giving it the big one. That's like the rule of the street anyway, but in prison you can't run if you want, or if a girl's bigger or ruder than you, so you have to go all out. You ain't got a choice; otherwise you end up getting targeted and then everyone's on your case. There's no way I was going out like that, fuck that. I'd rather fight back and get all my hair pulled out my head than sit there and get taken for a muppet. Don't get me wrong, I wasn't looking for trouble, I din't want stress, I just wan't gonna take no fuckeries from no-one - no matter who they were and where they were from. That's what was going around my mind: survival.

My cell mate, or pad mate, was named Diane and I can't remember her second name because I had a good few pad mates by the time I got out. Diane said everyone called her stumpy because she only had one arm.

I goes, 'Ain't that a bit disrespectful?'

She was like, 'I'm not bothered. People have called it me since primary school.'

I said I'd call her Di. I don't reckon she wanted to be called stumpy.

This is how I'd describe Di: Tall, skinny, with long, ginger hair and pale skin. She had flat boobs, a few freckles here and there, and one arm. It was her left arm that was missing, just past her shoulder, and she had a little stump that wiggled about when she was doing things like rolling a fag with her good arm or brushing her teeth. Di wasn't ugly, she just looked tired and worn out from taking too much brown and crack on the beat in Leicester, where she was born and bred. I liked her because she was different I suppose, not trying to act hard or nothing. Di was on remand for six-hundred pounds worth of shoplifted perfumes and bloke's t-shirts. She was walking back from Leicester town centre with all the stuff in a magic bag, which is like a big plastic shopping bag, but with layers of foil taped inside to fuck up the magnets in the shop security scanners, and the police pulled her over because they recognised her and knew how she made a living.

Di was like, 'Fuck it though, eh, it's not like they're going to life me off, is it?'

Which was true, she could only get a couple of months at the worst.

'Am doing my turkey as well, which is bait!' She said, pulling herself onto the top bunk mattress. Di obviously din't care about the piss and shit stains on it.

Doing turkey is cold turkey from heroin, the

withdrawal because you haven't had a hit for a day or two and it messes you up pretty bad. Di was already sniffling with her nose dripping and she kept going to be sick with note coming out. She was making horrible puking sounds and coughing up phlegm and all sorts. It was doing my head in, but I couldn't do ote, I had no choice, I just had to sit there and try and think of summat else when Di was having a good clear out of snot. I don't like stuff like that, people chewing loud right near me or picking their nose in front of me or snapping their toe nails. It can make me sick, so I just have to try and blank it out. Lads are worse for it most times, but being stuck in a shitty prison cell with a skinny smack head dry-puking, farting, and sniffling every two minutes is not a laugh.

Di was on DF's, DF118's, like withdrawal drugs that they give brown-head young offenders because they can't give them methadone. I don't think they were doing her any good though, she just kept going on about how she needed a dig and how sweet she'd feel if one of her mates on the unit could get her a little sorter of smack.

Di had been on remand before and served little sentences, what we called 'minor bird', so she told me the ins and outs of Glen Dale. Thanks to Di, I knew the score more or less straight away. Before we got talking proper though, Di stood at the window, with bars and thick glass, and shouted as loud as she could for her mate Claire Daniels. I'll always remember the name Claire Daniels because I couldn't help but piss myself laughing when Di was stood there screaming her name. This ginger smack-head with one arm shouting her head off from a prison window that you could barely breathe out of was funny, what-ya-call-it? Surreal. Di called to her mate for a good five minutes. I don't know why I was laughing, I just was.

'You're mad you are!' Di said. I told her I already knew that, but we were both smiling. Di was all good with me and we got on.

Eventually another girl shouted back about Di's

mate. Claire Daniels had been shipped out to another nick, basically transferred to another jail to finish her sentence. I can't remember what Di said, but she was pissed off.

'Maybe someone else has got gear?' I said.

Di din't have money in her prison spends account to pay for it, and she would end up getting in debt which wun't be good. At the end of the day she was just going to have to do her rattle, her cold turkey, and there was fuck all she could do about it.

It made me glad I wan't on smack or crack, but I could've done with a spliff to help me sleep that first night. Di showed me how to make my bed up like all the jail heads did theirs: the thick, green crab matt on the mattress to stop bugs and crabs and all that shit, then the thin green sheet goes down, tuck it in, then another thin sheet and two green, itchy blankets on top of that, and then you sleep in between the two sheets and with the blankets over you, but not touching your skin. There really were blankets with fleas on and it weren't good to let them touch you.

The itchy blankets reminded me of when we lived at Highwood House in St. Anns because we got kicked out of our home by the landlord. I can't remember why we had to leave, but the housing people put me, Sebella, Jade, and my mum in Highwood House until we got another yard. Highwood House is where all the poor families lived instead of being on the streets. We were given a small flat on the ground floor and it was alright really, except for the ants that were all over the place. Our blankets, like police station and prison blankets, were dead itchy and thin and you needed a good few of them to get warm. I had to keep my head and body under the covers, which me and Sebella nick-named 'itchy-bitchies', so the ants wun't get in and crawl over me. We used to get the big ants an all, the ones with wings and bigger bodies and it made me shiver when I woke up and they'd be crawling all over the bunk beds. It was horrible. You get used to it though, 'cause there ain't nowhere else to go, and I was ashamed to live there because everyone at school knew it was where poor families lived.

We stayed at Highwood House for months. It was around my tenth birthday, during Winter, because I've got the memory of riding fast on a BMX down Woodborough Road onto Huntingdon Street and into The Meadows to stay with my dad and his missis for my birthday weekend. When I was on my BMX I was free, in my head I was safe from anyone and nothing could stop me. I used to love freewheeling downhill.

Before we moved into Highwood House we were told by the housing bods that we would have to stay in a hotel until somewhere better was available. We were buzzing to be staying in a hotel: to us it was posh because we'd never been in a hotel before. It was The Park Hotel, next to the Arboretum, and as far as we were concerned it was the swankiest hotel in Nottingham. Fuck knows if it was one star or three, to us it was five stars. Clean sheets, clean carpets, a clean shower room, and a served breakfast. It was much nicer than what we were used to, but it only lasted one day.

We joined the local school, Windley, which has been knocked down now for flats and houses, and we only went there for one day, which is daft when ya think about it. We got introduced to the whole school and I spent the day telling boys I din't want to go out with them and making friends with a couple of girls, and we never went back. We moved into Highwood House the next day and joined the school nearest, which was Elms Primary, on Cranmer Street, St. Anns, same as Highwood. The only memory I've got of being at Elms was the day I rushed out of class and to the toilets, and before I could pull my knickers and skirt down, I shat myself. Runny, smelly poo was all over my legs and inside my knickers and skirt. It was even on my trainers. I was crying in the bogs as I cleaned myself up the best I could and then it was lunch time and the teacher sent another girl to check on me. I left the toilet thinking everything was all good and went and sat down for dinner and waited to be served by the head kid on the table. I looked down and there was a lump of shit on the back of one of my trainers. I had no excuse to go back to the toilet, so I sat there through the whole of lunch and waited 'til it finished and legged it to the toilet to clean the rest of the crap off my creps. I would have had the blood bullied out of me if any of the class had seen it. Thank fuck none of them did: young kids are cruel as anything.

When I had my induction at Glen Dale it was just me sat in a room, with a fresh looking male screw, watching a fifteen minute video about rules for youth offenders. The girls I came in with had all been locked up before, I was the only one who had to sit through the programme. The video was boring because Di had spent three hours the night before telling me all the rules of prison life. Don't leave the cell without tucking in your clothes and don't wear your flip-flops. Don't have your hair messy. Don't get tattooed and don't tattoo anyone else. There were literally hundreds of rules.

I wan't allowed a messy cell or to shout out the window or door, which prisoners did all the time. That got the Governor into trouble with locals who took him to court to calm us down. I shouted as long as I knew there were no screws around, creeping along the landing, listening for girls to place on report. I wan't allowed to throw a line out my door, which is when we got long, thin pieces of blanket and stuck a mirror or a comb to the end and slid it under the door onto the landing to catch on other lines to pass fags and stamps, drugs, or whatever was being swapped. We weren't allowed to shout out from the edges of our doors, where there was a little gap. Girls did it all the time and even some screws din't bother giving you a nicking sheet for it, which would get you stood in front of the Governor. A couple of the nob-head screws, the ones who must've been bullied when they were younger or been in the military and got shot at or blown up too much, would nick you any chance they got for the daftest thing, like accepting extra food at meal times from the girl in the cell next door, which the screws would say was bullying – even if it was your mate giving you two bits of stale bread. If the screw was a real wanker, and there was always a couple on each of the landings, then they'd stitch you up anyway they wanted or could get away with.

The first thing you learn in jail is the rules. The rules of the officers, the screws, e-they ew-scray, what they'll let you do, what they wont let you do, how to apply for visits from family or get brand new trainers sent in, and what-not. Then you learn the rules of the prisoners, the inmates, the jail-heads, rules that make survival bearable or hell, depending on if you learn quickly or not.

I've been street-wise almost from day one, so jail wasn't that much different when it came to keeping ma wits about me, watching what I said and to who, and being careful of who I knocked about with. If Di wan't ma pad mate, I probably wouldn't have bothered chatting to her, not because I'm that mad in the head or because she was a brown-head and had one arm, but because the other girls saw her as a cripple and weak and so it wouldn't have looked good for me to be best mates with her. Because she was my pad mate, it's different. When you're in a cell with another girl, you have to be like, what-ya-call-it? A unit: you have to work together to get through life each day. When we came in we got a little pouch of tobacco, and me and Di shared our fags so that it lasted a bit longer than if we just smoked them to ourselves. Like if it was scones with raisins and currants in, instead of giving it away to any old moo on the landing, I'd always give Di first refusal and she used to give me her jam doughnut because she din't like jam. She said it was too slimy. You have to share your stuff when you're living in a small space with another human, otherwise you'd just hate each other and go mental.

I've heard pad mates kicking the shit out of each other and it's not a nice sound. All kicking, punching, and shouting and everything getting clattered all over the place and it's fucked up because the screws don't know it's happening, and all the other girls on the landing start kicking their own doors and calling for the fighters to stop. That's if the two brawling cons are mates and friendly with everyone else. If no-one likes them they'd just let them kick ten barrels of shit out of each other.

14 Unhung

I had this one pad mate whose name I can't even remember: Cheryl or Kelly, a normal name, and she was one of the craziest girls I ever met.

I was on single bang up, in a cell on my own. I was at education in the afternoon and I came back and as soon as I got back onto the landing I heard a girl singing 'Old Macdonald' loudly from the side of a cell door. All the girls coming back from education started laughing because it ain't good to be singing out your door or window. The girls who were already locked up because they din't have jobs or ote must have bullied the girl to sing to give themselves some entertainment.

I shouted something like, 'Who's that singing then?' I must admit I was smiling and laughing a bit like everyone else.

Somebody recognised my voice and yelled out, 'What you laughing for Walters? It's your new pad mate!' A few people laughed even more then.

I went to my cell and opened the flap, what they call the observation flap, where screws look through, and there was a little girl, with the spottiest face I've ever seen, stood there singing.

'Stop fucking singing!' I ordered.

She went and sat down on one of the metal chairs. A screw came and let me in and goes, 'This is your new cell mate Walters,' he whispered to me, 'if anything happens to her, we'll blame you.'

He fucking meant it as well.

The door slammed shut and I stood there gawping at her. I asked her what her name was, but like I said I can't remember it so I'll say it was Kelly. She had a lesbian haircut, ya know like short, with no length at all and stuck to the head, like a bloke's trim, what a man or a dyke would have.

She was small, like five foot fuck all, and skinny with big boobs. Other than that she was just spotty, spottier than anything you've ever seen. I don't just mean acne, a few dots here and there. I mean angry, red bastards as well as yellow-heads that were seeping and large and disgusting to look at. She was always picking them, like proper pulling on 'em and squeezing 'em. She done one of the most horrible things I've ever seen: she had a shit and never washed her hands, then sat down and started picking a big bunch of red, puss-filled spots on her cheek. I wanted to puke.

I had to start telling Kelly the rules straight away. I was like, 'Don't ever sing out the window or door again, I don't care who shouts you and tells you to do it. I don't care if they threaten ya, don't do it.'

Kelly was unsure.

'I don't want anyone to get pissed off.'

I told her that at the end of the day it was my cell, and they'd have to come through me. I din't have a bad girl reputation or anything like it on the wing, girls knew what I was in for and knew I was a tool head and that's it. That means I use weapons if I have to. I'd defend Kelly if anybody came to the cell to trouble her, or if any gal shouted out the window or door to get her to do anything daft like sing or give her shit away on lines.

I couldn't defend her outside of the cell: each prisoner has to do it themselves. When it's coming to ya, ya gotta fight back straight away. That's a rule of the street as well, not just jail.

Everyone backed off from Kelly because I told them there wan't gonna be no more singing or bullying when she was in my cell. I had to act like that, as if I ruled the pad, otherwise they'd have had Kelly for lunch and made her more miserable than she was.

Kelly was what-d'ya-call-it? Manic depressed and suicidal: all she kept going on about was how she couldn't handle her sentence, which was four years for a robbery on an off-licence, and she wanted to kill herself. She even wrote a letter to her mum telling her she'd probably only come out of Glen Dale in a box. That was slack on her mum, you don't do that to ya family when they're already worried about ya. I told Kelly the score, just like Di had done to me. I told her how to survive, to not give up. For about a week, seriously, a good six or seven days, I was there going on and on about getting through it and being strong.

All Kelly wanted was to die; it's why she did the robbery on the off-licence in the first place. She was going to use the money to buy smack and overdose on a dig, a whole gram in one go. Even before prison she wanted to die and was depressed as ote. Once she jumped off a bridge that was over a train-track, but she din't die, she just fucked herself up, with bruises and a broken leg. The doctors put her on medicine, anti-depressives, and that din't help her, so she thought up her mad plan to do an armers, a robbery, on a shop and spend the money on committing suicide. Kelly got a knife from her mum's kitchen drawer, her dad's motorbike balaclava, and went to the off-licence in the village close to where she lived in some bumpkin place in Leicestershire, I don't remember where. She went and pulled the knife on the Asian guy running the place and he handed over three hundred quid, all the money in the till. The funniest thing about her planning it was the shop was one she used everyday, and she always wore the same clothes. The shop-keeper recognised her and told the police he thought it was Kelly. CID went 'round her house and found her there with two grams of heroin, rocks of crack, and a gram of coke. They arrested her for armed robbery: the courts gave her four years. As soon as she got to Glen Dale, Kelly slit open her wrists with a razor, but she din't do it properly and the nurses said it was attention seeking.

All Kelly talked about was doing herself in. It started to do my head in proper and it got to the point where I was like, 'Come on then, lets just get on with it!'

Kelly sat up on her grubby mattress, picking her spots and was like, 'What you on about?'

I said if she wanted to die then I'd help string her up on the window grid. I din't want her to die, I was just sick of her going on about it. I thought that if she had a taster of what it would be like then it might make her sort herself out and get on with her bird.

Kelly was up for it. We made a noose from a ripped up pillow case and tied one end around the top of the window and looped the other end so it went 'round Kelly's neck when she was stood on the chair under the grid. All she had to do was step off the chair. The plan was to let her hang for a minute or so and then I'd ring the emergency bell and pretend I was asleep and woke up and saw her swinging on the grid. They'd say I saved her and Kelly would know what it was like. I was secretly hoping that she would get some help from the doctors because part of me thought that Kelly needed extra care and attention.

It din't really go according to plan.

I can't remember what we said to each other, she stepped off the chair and started hanging. I'll never forget the look on her face as the noose tightened around her skinny neck. I'm not just saying this, her tongue came bursting out, like it was trying to slide out of her head and her eyes bulged, but they din't just bulge a bit, like if ya caught a lover with another person, they had all the life in them you've ever seen, I'm tellin' ya. She was looking right at me and I was stood still in front of her as her legs were going wild, not like in films when they twitch a little side to side. They were going crazy, kicking all over the place. Her face, which was obviously blotchy already 'cause of her spots, was pure red and getting bigger. Swollen, you'd say. Kelly was basically choking to death in front of me. The memory that sticks in my head the most, the one thing I'll never forget as long as I live, was the manic, bulging look of her eyes. They were staring at me, not even at me, right inside me, through me, locked on, as I stared back in shock. I knew what her eyes were saying. They were telling me, *I don't wanna be dead!*

Never mind ringing the bell, forget that, she'd have

been long gone before those lazy fuckers turned up. I grabbed her wild legs and lifted with all my strength, but obviously she's still choking 'cause the noose is tight as fuck round her neck, so I had to lift her, which was dead hard, believe me, and I din't know if she was going to make it. It was a struggle to lift her, but I managed to get her feet back on the chair and then I was still having trouble with the noose which was throttling Kelly. She was helping me untie it and eventually, after what seemed like ages but was only a minute or two, it came loose and Kelly dropped from the chair and threw the noose to the floor.

Kelly sat down and said, 'I din't like that, I din't like that at all.'

Her hands were shaking like a shitting dog's bones, I swear, and she started rolling a burn. I sat down on the chair opposite and said summat like, 'That was fucking mental!'

I rolled a fag an' all and couldn't take my eyes away from Kelly because she kept rubbing her neck and saying how horrible it was. We din't laugh. We sat there, each smoking and thinking. Kelly wun't look at me: she only looked at the floor.

Later we started going over it, what happened. It was one of the maddest things I've ever witnessed, I swear.

A few days later Kelly, or whoever she was, the suicidal maniac, moved out of my cell to go to another part of the prison and I gave her a hug and told her to be strong and survive.

15 Earning Stripes

The first trouble I had in Glen Dale was when I was still padded up with Di and about three or four weeks had gone by. I was getting used to the hours of bang up, about twenty-two per day, serious, and no-one had been to see me 'cause my mum couldn't afford the train or bus fair. I really missed Boo Boo Girl and Martin.

I was down the gym, playing a game of indoor hockey, with the yellow and blue plastic sticks and plastic ball and that. Normal hockey, running around, screaming and whacking the ball all over the place tryna score a goal. The thing is, I was actually good at hockey and I scored for the school team twice when they played me as a sub. Obviously nobody in Glen Dale knew that, so none of the captains picked me for their team. I was last to get picked, which was fair enough, they all knew each other and were mates. There was one girl, big and butch, and she was quite good, but she couldn't hack being tackled. She started getting grumpy if girls took the ball away from her. Half-way through the game the butch Mardy Arse had the ball and she sweated a couple of defenders easily, then she ran towards the corner of the sports hall to try and cross it to one of her mates waiting near the goal.

I legged it after her and stayed dead tight on her and pushed my stick round the side of her to try and knock the ball away. We were in the corner, and it was a concrete sports hall, we kept bumping into each other and battling our sticks for the ball. Mardy Arse din't like it and she stopped playing and turned around to push me in my tits. I fell back a bit.

Mardy Arse was like, 'Watch what ya fucking doing!' Her face was screwed up. She was an ugly cow as well, but she was way bigger than me, with chunky arms and legs. She wan't fat, just rounded, like chubby I suppose you'd say.

I goes, 'It's just a game, lets get on with it!' I din't want any trouble over a game.

Then she shouted, so everyone could hear, 'Don't start getting cheeky or I'll slap ya!' She came right up and in my face and we were clocking each other in the eye.

I wan't gonna back down, obviously, and I said summat along the lines of, 'Do what you want!'

She slapped me hard in the cheek.

It sounded loud in the big sports hall, with the echo and that and it hurt a little bit, but I just flicked my fist out and punched her right in her mouth. It was on then and she grabbed my hair with her left hand and I grabbed hers with mine and we swore at each other and started going punch for punch. Her bombs were stronger than mine, so I had to keep my head down because they were hurting. All the other girls were screaming for her to smash my head in, and the gym screws in the hall did nothing at first.

She kept hitting me on the side of the head 'cause my face was covered, and it fucking hurt. Each time her big fists landed, a white light flashed in my eyes. My punches were going all over the place, on her chin, on her shoulders, having hardly any effect at all. I started to go wobbly in my knees and she was still punching me and I was still trying, but I was done in and on my way to being knocked out properly. Just as piss was coming out my knickers and I was falling down the wall, a couple of bloke gym screws decided to step in to stop us. I was glad they did otherwise I'd have pissed myself in front of everyone.

The screw took me to an office to check me out. I had a black eye and loads of bumps on the left side of my head plus t-shirt marks where we'd been pulling each others' tops. The screw said we would both be getting nicked, which is when you go up in front of a Governor and get punished. I was told I could get my shower with the other girls, and as I got up I saw the butch girl I'd been fighting being taken away by an officer in uniform. She turned her chubby head back to look through the window of the office and we caught each others eye. She laughed at me and I walked away to get a shower.

I took my shorts, t-shirt, and knickers off and got into the shower block which was like a prison cell but instead with a door at each end, in and then out, with shower heads 'round the walls. The screws were dead tight about how long we could spend getting cleaned, so all the girls who played hockey or did weights or training had to cram into the space and get as clean as they could. There were twenty girls squashed under twelve showers, and they were chatting and laughing and getting on with soaping and washing themselves. When I walked in different girls started going on about the fight.

One of them said, 'Why din't ya just keep ya mouth shut and you wun't've got punched up?'

I was still dead full of emotion and had tears in my eyes, they couldn't see 'em 'cause of the steam though, so I din't say anything. They just kept laughing about how the girl did me in.

I waited two minutes to calm down and put my shower gel on my body and then I asked, 'What's her name anyway?'

A laughing girl, who was black and had a London accent, asked, 'Why d'ya wanna know?'

"Cause I'm gonna fucking stab the bitch!' I meant it as well, but they all started laughing all over again and a couple of them agreed that I'd better watch my mouth otherwise I could get done in there and then: they were obviously Mardy Arse's friends.

There was a tall girl, with long black hair and a slim body with tattoos on her arms and breasts, and she was stood across the shower room from me. She looked hard and her body was toned and she stood, well, like with confidence I guess. She stood confidently and I heard some of them call her Crawley when they were talking. Crawley looked at me and asked me where I was from.

'Notts.'

'Where abouts?'

'The Meadows.'

Crawley nodded. Another girl said I wasn't from The Meadows, but I ignored her, pretending I din't hear: because I din't roll there everyday din't mean I wan't from there.

Crawley smiled a bit and went, 'At least you stuck up for yourself and she's from your sides as well, Bulwell.'

'Oh,' I said, not too bothered; girls from Bulwell din't scare me.

'Where you from?' I asked Crawley.

'Lincoln. What you in for?'

'Section eighteen,' I replied.

More girls were laughing again and making noises like they din't believe me. Someone else asked what I did.

'I stabbed the bloke who raped my mate.'

'What with?' Asked the black girl from London.

'A knife,' I said.

A few chuckled again, mainly the black girl's mates and one of them said, 'You're getting a phat bird!'

Except Crawley, every woman in the shower laughed hard.

I kept looking at her and she seemed to ignore them. She was giving off vibes like she was on my side. She smiled at me and raised her eyebrows as if she was saying: *they're dumb bastards aren't they?*

I smiled back at her.

One of the gym screws shouted down the hallway that we had thirty seconds to finish off before the water went cold. Most of the girls had finished and there was me, a couple of skinny stragglers and Crawley. Then it was just me and Crawley. She walked up to me and whispered in my tab. She told me the name of the girl I had a fight with, she said her name was Deborah Donahue, or DD as a nickname. As we walked out of the shower room and into the changing room - which was like the ones you see at football grounds on television with benches 'round the sides and hooks on the walls - Crawley goes to me, 'You'll be alright. I'll look after ya.'

I got changed and din't speak to anyone else. My head was hurting, but I felt a bit better. By the time I got back to the wing around ten minutes later, all the girls and officers knew about the fight. Even Di, who was locked up all day, had found out. News travels fast in jail.

I kept going over it with Di, and she kept asking questions like did it hurt and how long did it last and where in the gym was it and which part of her mouth did my punch land. I think Di was excited by it because it was actually her own pad mate that had taken part in the fight that the whole nick knew about, especially as it was with Deborah Donahue, who everyone had heard of. Obviously DD had a reputation in the jail and I figured out that's why she couldn't take me tackling her in front of all the other prisoners, because she din't want them thinking she couldn't play.

Di was like, 'It's good that you had a go though, people will think twice before they fuck with you, even DD's mates.'

I must admit, I wanted them to know they couldn't fuck with me and get away with it. I wanted to be known for giving it as good as I got, even if I blatantly din't win, that din't matter. As long as they knew I'd fight back. Plus I had Crawley backing me.

When I asked Di if she'd heard of Crawley, she straight away answered, 'Yeah, of course! She's dead hard. Once she punched a screw in the face and broke his nose. She's always banged up for fighting and robbing.' Crawley had a reputation as well, which made me feel good.

I lay on my bed, thinking over and over about the fight, cussing myself for not doing better and not winning. No-one could have baited me if I'd have knocked DD out. I started fantasising about revenge. It made my heart beat faster and I had to stand up and walk around the cell because I was rushing off it so much. The screws gave us cheap, yellow razors to shave our legs and armpits and I got one of mine and stamped on it a few times to break the blade out. I got my plastic fork and bent the head of it and snapped it away so it was just the handle. I grabbed Di's lighter and stood near the window. She wondered what I was up to and I told her to watch. I started burning the end of the broken fork where the fork bits used to be attached and it caught fire and wisps of black smoke floated up and plastic was dripping to the floor. When it was burning good I grabbed the little blade which was on the window sill and blew the flames out. As soon as the flame went out I squashed half the razor into the soft, melted plastic and used the edge of the lighter to shove the blade further in. I was blowing on it loads when it was in place, and because the plastic goes hard again quick, the blade set in. I stood there next to the open window, holding my new tool and smiling.

Di said, 'You're mad you are. What ya gonna do with it?'

I was like, 'Slash that fucking DD, that's what I'm going to do with it!'

Di was saying I shun't do it, I was barmy, it would get me more time, I'd never get out, blah blah blah, all that lot.

I couldn't get it out of my head. Revenge on DD was all I could think about. It's like with Henley, once I got it in my head to do him, I had to follow through. I wan't fucking about. It's like when I was growing up down The Meadows and older or bigger girls used to force me to eat sweets that'd been on the ground, or nick chocolate bars from the Co-op in the precinct, all I could think about was growing up, finding the bullies and hurting them. That might sound mad, like you wun't think I'd do it, but that's how it gets ya. It grows in ya head. Nowadays I don't give a shit about those bullies, growing up is growing up. One of 'em's doing a life sentence anyway.

With DD, the big, dumb bitch from Bulwell, it was different. I saw myself as the person to teach her a lesson once and for all.

I tested the fork blade on my pillow, which I got Di to hold in front of her and I was pissed off because on the second slice down it the blade snapped off. It cut through the pillow case, but din't mark the sponge underneath. That gave me a fresh idea.

I got my plastic spoon and snapped off the scooping end, so I had just the handle. I spent fucking hours sanding it down against a chip in the concrete on the window sill. I shaped the end into a sharp point. Di had to stand at the cell door to tell me when anyone was walking past or coming to the flap. Girls used to come round begging for bits-and-bobs, like stamps and burn, and if they knew what I was doing word would spread. The last thing I wanted was the screws finding out I was making weapons, and I definitely din't want DD to know. Di was keeping watch for me, nervous as shit, like she was on the look out of her first burglary, and I worked the end of the spoon into a proper shank, that's what they call prison knives. Shanks, chivs, shivs, blades, whatever: I think those names came from American jails, which are ten times rougher than our nicks and they have all kinds of mad weapons.

This time when I grabbed the pillow and rammed the new tool into it, it stabbed right through each time. I did it about twelve or thirteen times. I could tell it was a dangerous tool and my heart was beating all crazy.

I kept picturing DD's ugly face as I was stabbing the plastic into her ribs, puncturing her lungs, jukking her throat and cheeks. I was thinking of all the ways I could fuck her up.

Di said I was loony. I din't give a shit what she thought. I had like, one vision, you know, what they'd call tunnel vision, I suppose. I wasn't thinking of my future, of all the different things that could happen. I was still young and had my dreams of being a famous girl rapper at number one in the charts. Being in prison keeps you alert, some seriously fucked up shit can happen if ya not careful, so worrying about the years ahead of me din't even come into it. I needed to concentrate on surviving and not getting taken for a ride.

If you weren't on the ball, you never knew when something was going to come up and maybe mess you up for the rest of ya days. People on the street would probably say that girl's jails aren't rough, but it's not the truth.

16 Wainwright

Before I got my revenge on DD for humiliating me, an incident happened on our wing involving a girl called Amanda Wainwright.

I was still getting used to being locked up and learning who was who and what was what - there was loads to learn and Di was telling me everything she knew - so I din't know which gangs were which; who was running things on the unit; who was the toughest and that lot.

One day on association I just finished putting the phone down, probably after speaking to Martin or Boo Boo, I can't remember, and straight away saw about six girls going into the toilets near the showers, which were away from the association room in a little hallway. I could tell something hot was going down because all the girls rushed in there quickly and were looking around them to clock if any screws were about.

The leaders of the little crew were two girls going out with each other called Natasha and Michelle. Everyone called 'em Natty and Chelle. Di said they went everywhere together and shared a cell as well. Natty was a tall black girl with big hair and a big arse and she always had on about four or five gold sovereign rings, ear rings and a couple of gold necklaces. She always wore expensive Nike trainers, always the top make. Chelle was small, more like Boo Boo's size, five foot four or summat, and she had blonde hair that was always in a pony tail and she was white. Chelle din't have no gold or rings or ote, but she was pretty. They were both pretty.

They ran a little clique on the wing, not with a name like the Crips or Bloods or the 10 Tigers or anything like that, it was just called Natty's gang because they all did everything she said.

Natty's gang were like her joey's and bunch of slaves

because she was on remand for murder and they were all scared of her. She was the first murderer I'd ever seen in real life and I must admit I was wary of her.

Di told me about the murder Natty committed.

Natty's boyfriend, I cant remember his name, was a crack dealer who was making loads of money in a rough area in Leicester, it might have been Highfields, and he was out raising all the time and doing okay for them both. He arranged a deal one day and the three fiends turned up at his flat - where he was living with Natty - wanting around four-hundred pounds worth of crack from him. When Natty's boyfriend started cutting up the rocks and weighing them, he caught one of them trying to sly some of the chunks off the table and he jumped up, slapped the fiend, finished the deal, and told them to get the fuck out of his house and don't ever come back. About an hour later loadsa lads rush the flat and start stomping on Natty's boyfriend, proper tooling him up because they had bats and knives and all sorts. The fiend that got slapped was there as well. There was a massive gang of them, all tooled-up, masked-up and going mental, ransacking the place.

Natty ran to the kitchen screaming for them to leave her man alone and she grabbed a knife from the drawer and ran back to the front room where she started stabbing them left, right and centre. Natty stabbed three of them while they were beating her bloke up. They all ran away and one of them that she hit fell in the road, just below the window to Natty's flat. His mates ran off and left him: he died there and then in the street. The worse thing for Natty was that her own boyfriend told the police that the stabbings weren't nothing to do with him, that Natty did 'em, and because two of the other guys she stabbed gave statements against her she was up for murder and section eighteen assault. It's fucked up really.

Natty tried to defend her man, she even stopped them from battering him, and all he did was sell her out. She was looking a big bird for nothing. It went to Natty's head though, I think she was too young to understand it all and realise how fucked she was. She used to shout at people when she was angry with them, 'I'll fucking kill ya like I killed that guy!' Shit like that, like she was proud of it. I stabbed a bloke too, but I reckon I had a good reason. I still wun't gonna go round bigging myself up, at least not in anyone's face anyway. People start to hate ya when ya do that.

On the day I watched Natty's gang going into the toilets, I wondered what they were up to, so I walked over to the bogs and went in. They were crammed into one cubicle, so I sat in the next one and listened.

I could hear Natty, she was going mad at a girl they had trapped in there. Natty was like, 'Just tell me what you've got, giz some of it and we'll be all good with ya, don't fucking lie!'

I could hear the rest of the gang saying the same thing and the girl they had hold of was saying shit like, 'Honestly, I ain't got ote, I swear down Natty, it was just ma brother come to see meh, he din't bring me note, I swear!' Natty was getting all vexed and I could hear them all punching and slapping the girl as she was begging to be let go.

Natty went, 'Right, bring the slag upstairs now!' They dragged her out the bogs and I followed them. On the way up the stairs behind them, I clocked the girl they had taken and saw that she was a skinny smack-head type, with scabs and greasy hair: she looked a fucking mess.

One of the nosey girls on the wing, Clarkey, who knew everything about everyone, came up to me and asked what was going on. I told her that Natty's gang had kidnapped someone.

'Was it Wainwright?' Clarkey asked.

I din't know if it was or not, but Clarkey was suddenly not interested anymore and was too scared to come with me upstairs when I asked her to. I went to the three's landing where I found Wainwright's cell. I walked up to it and opened the observation flap a little and saw the gang had Wainwright held down on her bed. Two of the gang had her arms pressed down above her head, one pushed her waist down, and two others had her legs wide open like a doctor does when he checks a girl out or she's having a baby. Wainwright was struggling a bit, but not half as much as I woulda been.

I'd have been like a wild animal.

While they held her down, Natty leaned over and pulled Wainwright's tracksuit trousers and knickers down to her ankles and pushed her fingers into her fanny. Wainwright started struggling more and crying and begging to be let go. I'll never forget the look on her face, like she was being poisoned. Tears were falling off her face, but she couldn't stop them. They were punching her and whacking shampoo bottles off her face and body and one of 'em smacked her with a prison ashtray. Natty pushed her fingers right inside Wainwright and at first I couldn't figure out what they were doing to her. Chelle, who was stood next to Natty and was punching Wainwright loads, was like, 'If there's smack up there we're fucking having it you bitch!' Wainwright was crying and was obviously in pain because Natty still had her rings on and was forcing her hand into her fanny, right inside. You don't have to be a square-head to know that would hurt. I felt sick watching and wanted to kick off on them, but I would've got my head battered and it would've started more shit than I needed, but I wanted to, because it's like they were raping her, ya know, proper fucking violating her.

Just for drugs.

Chelle turned round and saw me at the flap and went, 'You better fuck off now!'

I turned and walked away, back down the landing. When I got to the top of the landing stairs I could still hear what was going on. I felt horrible and I couldn't do anything about it.

I was hyper, my heart pumping like mad and I kept

thinking about what I could have done to stop them from abusing Wainwright. She din't do anything to anyone and they were bullying her because they could, they had the power.

I went back to my cell and told Di what happened. Di said it was a normal thing to happen if they thought you had drugs inside you, smuggled in from a visit or chucked over the fence. Natty and Chelle and the rest of the gang regularly held girls down and searched their bodies for smack. I thought maybe one day I would settle the score for Wainwright, but right then I had my own shit to deal with.

There were two days 'til the next hockey session when I'd catch up with DD.

17 Crawley

The day after Wainwright got pinned down, I went in the showers, got naked and started to clean myself when the door opened and Crawley came in holding her kit. I was happy to see her, so I smiled and said hello.

Crawley looked like she din't know me and her face was puzzled for a second, then it clicked and she remembered, 'Oh it's you,' she laughed a bit, 'DD's mate!'

I laughed an' all, hoping she was still okay with me.

Crawley walked like nothing bothered her. She took her clothes off and stood near one of the benches undoing her ponytail as if it was her own bathroom. Being naked, when anyone could have walked in, din't bother her. Confidence, I suppose, that's what you'd call it. Crawley showed confidence. When she wasn't looking towards me I glanced at her boobs and tattoos and had to look away quickly. I looked at her pussy as well. I felt like a pervert, but I wanted to look at her. There was something about Crawley that I liked.

I'm not a lesbian, I already said that: I was secret bi. I knew I was bi ever since I used to get prickly and tickly feelings in my arms when Mrs Melton used to sit next to me to correct my home work or look at my drawings. I loved getting attention from Mrs Melton. Once, outside of school I saw her walking her black and white dog, like a sheep dog, along the river and I ran over to her and walked with her and even threw the smelly yellow ball for her dog, I can't remember its name, and I felt great. When Mrs Melton said she had to go home she told me she was looking forward to seeing me the next day in school and I was so happy I skipped all the way home, jumping up and down and acting all giddy. I had a crush on her.

With Crawley I din't feel like that straight away, I just knew I wanted to be around her. I was so glad there were no other girls in the shower. It's little moments that help you in a lonely place like jail. Anytime you make a connection with a person on a good level - a person who you're safe with – it makes your bird okay and you can have a laugh and it don't get you down as much.

When Crawley got into the showers, she used the one next to mine, she could have chosen any of 'em but she chose to be next to me.

I was still a bit embarrassed about being naked in prison around people who I din't know. Me, Valerie, and Boo Boo Girl were always starkers around each other, trying on each others clothes and all that, but it took a bit of getting used to in jail. It's one of those things you have to deal with and get numb to after a while.

Crawley started rubbing shower gel on her body and I put shampoo in my hair. After about a minute she asked me my name.

'Walters.'

'I mean your proper name, ya first name?'

I told her it was Stephanie and she said it was her cousin's name. I asked her what her name was. Zoe.

Zoe Crawley.

'You're in for stabbing someone aren't ya?' She asked, just as she was standing under the shower and the bubbles and creamy gel ran down her body and legs.

One of the tattoos on Crawley's arm was the words, BEEN THERE DONE THAT, which I thought was funny, like a cheeky thing to have on ya.

I told her that I stabbed up a rapist after me and my mate Valerie kidnapped him.

'Good,' Crawley said, 'I fucking hate nonces.' I agreed with her.

'What did you do?' I asked.

'Cash point robbery.'

I asked her what happened.

'Robbed a bloke at a NatWest cash point in Lincoln. My ex grabbed him from behind after he'd put his pin number in and they were fighting, and I ran up and withdrew two hundred quid. Got caught a couple of days later because of the CCTV. Hot move. Stupid.' She let the water go over her head and face. I watched the water run down her curves.

'What do you reckon you'll get?'

'About three or four years.'

I was like, 'Ya what? That's harsh!'

'Not really,' she said, smiling. 'I got three years last time for beating up a taxi driver, and I was with my ex that time as well. He's just got six years for this. He's a dick anyway.'

That made me laugh, the way Crawley said certain words. She had a nice voice.

I asked her why she hadn't been sentenced yet but her ex-boyfriend had. She told me that her ex pleaded guilty because he broke the bloke's jaw and Crawley was hoping to get her charge reduced from robbery to theft if she took it to a trial. If the charge was lowered then she could only get about two years, maximum, and she'd already done four months on remand.

We talked about our cases and the sentences we were looking and I learned a few new things about Crawley, like she was in and out of care homes and prisons since she was thirteen. She was twenty when I met her. Crawley'd had a rough life, like Valerie, but she seemed smarter than Val, like she was clever and she was prettier and friendlier as well.

Crawley asked me how I felt after my fight with DD. I told her it pissed me off and I wanted to deal with her. I told her I wanted to rush DD.

Crawley laughed a bit and looked at me.

'You're mad aren't ya?'

'What do ya mean?'

'One of them psycho bitches!' Crawley laughed again, but in a nice way.

I was a bit embarrassed.

'Of course I'm not. I just want to get her back.'

'What ya gonna do?' She asked.

'I'm gonna stab the cow!'

This time Crawley laughed loud and it echoed around the shower room. Her voice was like a happy mother's laugh, if ya know what I mean. I did feel a little p'd off that she din't believe me, so I told her I'd done it before and I din't give a fuck about doing it again.

'That's the point though, init Stephanie? You don't have to do it. Leave it to me: I'll get DD for ya.'

'What?' I said, shocked. 'No it's alright, I'll do it myself. People will think I can't fight my own battles.'

Crawley goes, 'But you can't though can ya? Ya got beat up!'

She kept laughing and moved out of the shower to her clothes and grabbed her towel.

'Look,' she goes, 'don't worry about it. I don't like DD anyway and never have done. I'll punch her up when I see her and make out it's about something else, ok?'

I felt too daft, to baited, to say anything.

I din't want Crawley's charity 'cause I knew I could get DD back.

As she was drying herself, Crawley said, 'Come up to my pad when ya done and I'll show ya summat yeah?'

I din't know what she was on about, but I told her I'd go to her cell as soon as I'd done drying my hair.

Then she got herself ready, still with her own long hair drenched, and fucked off.

I liked Crawley, I wanted to get to know her, but what she said pissed me right off. I'm tellin ya, I knew I wasn't gonna allow DD to walk 'round thinking she had one over me. Fuck that. I was going to tell Zoe, Crawley, I was gonna tell her I could deal with DD on ma todd.

I dried myself quickly, got dressed into the prison tracksuit and went upstairs to find Crawley's cell somewhere on the three's landing. I had to ask a couple of girls hanging around on the top of the stairs which pad was Crawley's. It was at the end of the landing next to the fire escape. I walked down thinking of what I was going to say - *Crawley, I don't want you involved, I'll deal with it myself, thanks for the offer but I'm all good* - that type of shit.

I arrived at Crawleys cell, number 3-14, I think, and pushed open the door to look inside.

Crawley wasn't there.

I walked inside and looked around. I couldn't believe how much stuff she had and she was in a single cell on her own, with a single bed and a proper wooden chair and table; not like the shitty metal ones we had coming out the walls. She also had a set of shelves and a black television. I knew any of us could have a TV in our pad, but we had to be well behaved and on enhanced regime which gave us more privileges. At that stage I was on standard regime, which is what most girls were on. Crawley had a rug and quilt cover, both of 'em light blue. She'd made curtains by attaching a green prison sheet above the window and splitting it up the middle with a razor and tied each side back with pieces of string. On her table she had loads of toiletries laid out; shampoos, perfumes, soaps, creams, all sorts; brand new tubes of toothpaste and under-arm deodorants, talcum powder and sponges. In jail ways she was phat - her cell was plush. Crawley had everything she needed and a bit extra. I must admit, I was impressed.

There were photographs on the wall above her bed; a large, round woman hugging Crawley in a back garden; an old man sat next to a canal; two kids in a bubble bath and one blurry one showing Crawley looking all done up in a white dress, like on a night out, hair squeezed with straighteners and make up on, laughing with three of her mates and pulling daft faces.

Crawley turned up at the door and said summat like, 'I hope ya ain't nicked ma burn!'

I smiled. 'Course not, I'm just looking.' I pointed at her friends and family and she told me who they were.

The fat woman was her mum. The old guy was her dead granddad. The kids were her son Josh and her daughter Kelsey who both lived with Crawley's mum most of the time.

'Sit down if ya want.' I sat on the middle of the bed.

Crawley pulled a spliff from somewhere and was like, 'I'll twos you up on this if ya like?'

I went, 'Yeah, of course.' It was the first spliff I'd had in jail and I'd been inside for a month.

We blew the thick smoke out the window and when one of us was blazing the other checked the landing for screws. It was only a small hash joint and was gone after about two minutes. I started to feel stoned straight away and I saw in Crawley's mirror that my eyes were getting hazed and my cheeks were going red. My mouth went dry and I did feel a bit weird, like a bit para' about getting found out. Looking out at the prison fence and barbed wire din't make me feel wicked, but I styled it out and told Zoe I felt dan. That's when she said I talked like rude-girls.

I said, 'It's just city speak.'

After a couple of minutes of sorting her bits-and-bobs, like putting her shower gel and shampoo back in order and folding her soaking towel around the radiator pipe, Crawley grabbed her stereo from under the bed. It was a grey CD player type thing, like ones ya always see, Phillips or Sony, not a dead expensive one but a decent one. Zoe took the back off it and sat on the bed next to me. She took out the six batteries, chunky ones, R20's they call 'em, and stretched her arms to her cupboard without getting up and grabbed a pair of prison socks. She got a sock in her hand and put four R20's in it and placed that sock inside the other one.

'Here,' she said, 'smash DD over the head with these.'

Crawley was serious, no smiling.

My heart was racing. I took hold of the home made tool and wrapped the end of the sock around my right fist for a strong grip.

'When should I do it?' I asked.

'Tomorrow: after hockey.'

18 DD

As I held the heavy weapon, one of the girls that were stood at the top of the stairs shouted, 'Screw on the landing!'

Crawley picked up her talcum powder and blasted loads around the cell and opened the windows as far as they'd go. She told me I'd better do one, so I looked in the mirror, tried to put on a straight face and went back to my pad.

I took the batteries in the socks with me.

I lay down on my bed, Di was talking, but I wasn't really listening. I was red and wanted to be left alone to be in my head. I was thinking about the showers and Crawley. I thought about what we said and pictured it all again. Watching her body. Smoking the spliff. Looking at her photos. Sitting on her bed and checking out the weapon, holding it in my hand.

Crawley obviously liked me. Why, though? That's what I wanted to know. I cun't figure out what was so special about me. I was getting on with my bird like everyone else. I want even thinking about getting sentenced, I don't know why.

I was missing Boo Boo, I was missing walking around, going where I wanted to, having cash in my pocket, snorting a line of billy, shocking out to tunes, all that lot, but I was surviving jail, so I din't think loads about not being on the street, or 'on the out' as people banged up call the real world. Don't get me wrong, as soon as I got my sentence I soon started missing life and got all wounded about being behind bars, but just then, on remand, on my bed stoned and glowing inside, I was only on a tip about one thing for certain: fucking up DD the next time I saw her.

I din't show Di the tool, but I told her I was doing DD in the next day at gym, in the changing rooms. Di wasn't down with it and she tried to talk me out of it. I couldn't back down. There was no red light. I wouldn't have been able to get DD out of my head if I din't get revenge.

Di was one of those girls that were so different from most people, 'cause she only had one arm - she avoided trouble like fighting and all that. Most of the time people started on her and she just left 'em to it. I wasn't brought up like that; no-one down The Meadows was brought up like that. Ya had to fight other kids to play on the park at the bottom of Arkwright Walk, because if you din't, ya wun't be able to go anywhere except the back garden. I don't know if that made me a nutter or whatever, but I had to show DD. I had to teach her a lesson. I wanted her to look in the mirror and think, *I shun't have messed with that Stephanie Walters because I've never got a beating like she gave me.* DD would think twice before she went 'round bullying smaller girls just because they're better than her at something.

I started to gear myself up, going through the types of attacks I could deal with. My heart was pounding like crazy, even when I was cotched on my bed. That's how violence gets ya; think about it long enough and it takes over.

The next day I got my name on the list for hockey in the afternoon and checked with Crawley that she was coming too. I was buzzing that she said she would watch my back and make sure no other girls stepped in to help DD.

Di had a health care appointment, or 'MO's' as they call it inside, to get cream for her stump because it got itchy and flaky and whatever. I spent all morning in the pad on my own, practicing swinging the sock full of massive batteries against my pillow that I wedged against the window.

I kept wondering what DD was doing there and then, like rolling a fag or writing a letter or chatting out the window. Crawley told me that DD always went to hockey when it was on, so I din't have to worry about her not turning up.

When it was lunch I nearly couldn't eat ote because of what I was going to do. I was glad I was going to do it, it was the nerves giving me butterflies and I couldn't even have a little nap. I lay on my bed, working myself up. There was no way I wasn't going to do it. I couldn't back down.

When they did let out for hockey I had the batteries in the socks in my gym towel, with clean knickers and socks, rolled up neat so the screws couldn't tell there was anything different about my kit compared to any other girls. I was shaking a bit, getting dry mouth and all that. I waited for Crawley outside the main doors of the wing but I couldn't see her and the SO told me to stop hanging around and get to gym or he'd lock me in my cell. I slowly walked towards the gym, which was down loadsa long corridors, and then you had to go outside across a small field and it was there. The chapel was next to it and there was another field behind it as well. That's where we played rounders and football or ran. There were lots of girls going into the gym and I still couldn't see Crawley or DD.

As soon as I got inside the changing rooms I saw Crawley standing in the corner and she said 'Eh, up', so I went over to her and a couple of her mates. She asked me if I had the batteries and I tapped my towel. Crawley smiled and told me DD was already in the sports hall getting ready to play.

I got changed next to Crawley and her mates and we all went into the hall and a screw came and we picked teams and started playing.

DD was there and she din't look at me or anything, I heard her laughing a couple of times and I'm sure she was on about me. I still felt nervous, but I really wanted to get her back, so I held it down and acted like nothing was going on. We even ended up clashing sticks, like nearly tackling each other all over again and we din't talk to each other and I din't really look at her. I din't want her to see my eyes. We all played like nutters for about an hour and then the gym screw told us to get a shower and be ready to get back to the wings.

I felt knackered, my legs were tired, my hair was stuck to my face, and sweat was dripping down my back. My lungs were hurting like mad. I felt weak. I still had to do what I had to do. I was walking out of the sports hall when Crawley jogged up to me and said, 'Let DD get in the showers first, then when she's drying herself, deal with it yeah?'

'Yeah, yeah. I will do, safe.'

I was last into the changing rooms and I sat down on the bench and watched the other girls piling into the showers. Everything was normal. There were dozens of girls laughing and shouting. A couple of them came out and started to get dry, but there was no sign of DD. I sat there with my rolled up towel on my knees with the end of the socks full of batteries sticking out. I waited and watched. There were no gym screws in the changing rooms, and I got up with the towel and tool and walked over to the door and looked across at the office. Two male gym screws were sat down chatting. I turned around and a load more girls were coming out of the showers. There was steam in the air and puddles all over the floor.

It was still normal.

A few more seconds or summat like that and Crawley comes out of the showers with her towel round her body, pointing at herself and moving her mouth. That was her saying that DD was coming behind her.

Crawley sat down and DD walked into the changing room in her towel. I watched her walk over to a corner, sit down and start talking with her mate. DD din't look up. The room was getting busier and louder and I was stood there, the only person still in shorts and t-shirt. My heart was beating like mad. I looked at Crawley and she was drying her legs and looking at me, mouthing to me, 'Go on!'

It was now or never.

I unrolled my towel, clocking every girl in there, making sure no-one saw what I was up to. I wrapped the end of the sock around my right fist and started walking towards

DD who was still drying herself and not looking up. I stood in front of her and noticed her cronies on either side looked up. I quickly lifted the tool high, swung it down and the batteries cracked off DD's head, the sound was like a pool ball being hit. She made a little noise and her body jumped. She looked in my eyes.

I hit her again, two quick smacks, making her drop her towel. DD stood up and put her arms out, pure dazed. I cracked her again and blood trickled down her forehead. DD jabbed at me, she was wobbly and confused, I smacked her again, splitting a fresh cut that started dripping blood near her ear. I could hear girls screaming.

'Leave her alone!'

'Come on DD!'

A gym screw behind me shouted, 'Drop the weapon and stand back', but DD was still trying to fight and flapping all over the place, like an injured goose. I dashed back on my toes a little and swung the socks twice, like I'd practised in my cell, connecting on her head both times. She looked like she was gonna collapse and I was expecting the screws to rush me any second. I dropped the tool and walked towards the door, smiling like a fruitcake. The rest of the girls could not believe their eyes, and most of 'em DD's mates. A big gym screw grabbed my arm and said summat, but I wan't listening. I looked around and a woman screw was helping DD to walk with her arm under DD's shoulder. There was blood coming from three or four different cuts, running down her face and neck. She looked fucked up, gutted that she'd just been done in. The big gym screw dragged me into the office and the last thing I heard was one of DD's mates saying I was a dead bitch.

I was buzzing and smiling and right then and there I din't give a fuck about any of 'em. I just battered one of the hardest out of all of them, so what the fuck was they gonna do?

Fuck all, they're just talkers.

The screw sat me down and started asking me why I

did it, and why I din't stop when he shouted. I said to ask DD about why, and I din't stop because I din't want to. DD deserved it.

The gym screw's like, 'She could be seriously injured.'

I'm like, 'So fucking what?'

The screw got all pissed off, so he rang the security screws and locked me in the office on my own.

I sat smiling.

I was in trouble with the jail, but glad I got DD back for punching me up. That's what starting my prison time was about: learning the score, showing people they couldn't fuck with me and get away with it.

Now it's all different, but then it was all about surviving, growing up, getting out my anger. I was a teenage girl all over the place, going with the flow, wanting to fit in, wanting a reputation, and all that lot.

I was returned to the wing without having a shower or even being allowed to change out of my gym clothes. They put me in my cell and told me I was being nicked for assaulting another prisoner. I was banged up for a couple of days until I had to see the Governor and get my punishment. Girls kept coming to the door, asking me what happened and why I did it. Most of them couldn't believe it was DD that got done in. I was bigging myself up, saying stuff like, 'Well she shun't fuck about should she?'

Di couldn't believe it either. She kept saying I was going to get in more shit if I carried on. I liked Di, she was a safe girl, but she was bummy. She wan't used to sticking up for herself with violence like I was. I wanted people to know that they had to watch me, I admit it, fuck it. I had enough anger inside me if girls wanted to mess about. I wan't really scared of no-one, I'm not just saying that. I honestly wan't bothered if a girl was bigger or stronger than me, I could still hit her with a tool or pour boiling water over her head or something. At the end of the day, unless they were going to knock me out or blast me, then I was going to put up a fight and do what I had to do to protect myself. Like with DD, if ya beat me up, I'll come back for you. I wan't like Valerie though, fighting blokes and that, but anyone can be tooled up can't they? That's the way it is. It's mad.

19 The Block

Two days after I smacked up DD, a screw took me to 'the block', which was what they called the punishment wing. I was put into a cold, stinky cell. It din't hardly have ote in it; a metal toilet and sink with all kinds of piss and shit on; a window with grids and bars and a metal bed frame with no mattress. That was it. No table, no chair, nothing; just the bog, sink, and metal bed. The smell of the toilet was rank and most of the time while I was waiting I stood near the window gulping in as much air as I could. I din't like that cell at all, it was gammy as anything and I couldn't even sit down because the floor was layered in dust, pubes, nubs, and all sorts of stains. I din't realise prison cells could be that disgusting. I had to wait a good couple of hours as well, and when they came for me I was grateful to get away from that cell.

That's the maddest thing, when you're in jail, the whole place is shit. Ya locked away in crappy rooms and cells and everywhere has that prison smell and most places need a clean, but then you get the cells, toilets, and showers that are just fucking bait as you like. Shit-holes, like my mum used to say: places you wun't keep a scabby cat.

The Governor that dealt with me and DD was a mean bastard. He looked it an' all. He had one of those red faces like alcoholics have and a moustache that was dead thick. He had brown hair with bits of grey in it and he looked quite stocky even though I couldn't tell properly because he was sat down. He was Welsh and din't smile once. He was sat behind a wooden desk, a big HMP Glen Dale sign behind him on the wall. There were a couple of filing cabinets and another little table with a kettle, tea bags, and cups on, close to where I was stood. There was a chair on each side of the Governor's table for screws to sit on.

DD was already stood in front of the Governor, with a screw next to her, and I was told to stand about a meter away from her while the screw that brought me in stood between us. There weren't no chairs for us, the Governor told us to stay standing and then he was like, 'You girls have a history of getting in one another's way, so I'm warning you now: any more trouble in front of me or my officers and I'll keep you down here for a month.'

I couldn't imagine living for a month in that gammy cell.

'Is that clear?'

'Yes,' we answered.

'When you address me, say, "Yes Governor!"'

'Yes Governor,' we replied at the same time.

The Governor turned to one of the screws, 'There are two incidents to deal with today, correct?'

The screw said yes and started to read from a piece of paper in his hand.

'Governor, on the twentieth of this month, at approximately three pm in the gymnasium, PSI's stationed in the gym witnessed inmates Walters and Donahue fighting, namely punching and slapping each other, and called for them to stop. Neither inmate did as they were instructed and the officers eventually intervened and split them up. None of the officers witnessed who started the fight. Both Walters and Donahue were punching.'

The whole time the Governor is staring at us like he wants to kill us.

'Also, on the twenty-seventh of this month, also in the gymnasium, time not recorded actually, officers stationed in the gym witnessed inmate Walters assaulting inmate Donahue with a crude weapon fashioned from prison property, namely a sock filled with batteries. Inmate Walters was ordered to stop on two occasions but ignored officers' shouts. Donahue suffered various cuts and bruises about her head and face and was treated with butterfly stitches by the medical officer.'

The screw pulls out the sock with batteries from under his chair and plonks it on the Governor's table. The

Governor grabs the tool and he's holding it, moving it about, and getting a feel for it. He's looking at me and then he's like this, 'Would you like to be hit with this?'

'No.'

'What gives you the right to hit another person with it?'

I thought, *fuck this idiot*, so I said, 'I don't care.'

His eyes went wild and he screamed, 'You will care! You will care right now!'

I goes, 'No I won't actually.' Even DD laughed a bit.

The Governor slammed the tool down on the table, like he was using it on someone, and went, 'Get her out of my sight!'

One of the screws grabbed my arm and pulled me out of the room and put me back in the horrible cell and told me I should have kept my mouth shut. I din't say anything back to him and he slammed the door and walked off. I went over to the window to get some fresh air.

After about twenty minutes the screw came back and took me in front of the Governor again. DD wan't there and it was just the Governor and the screws. I pleaded not guilty to the fight with DD because I said she started it, which she did.

'Well, I've found you guilty,' the Governor said.

I frowned. I din't even get a chance to argue my side of it. I pleaded guilty to tooling DD up and the Governor gave some daft speech about me being against authority and a trouble-causer and how he would ship me off to a proper jail like Holloway if I din't buck up my ideas. I let him say whatever he wanted to say, and then he gave me my punishment.

For the fight he gave me seven days CC, cellular confinement, and for tooling up DD he gave me forty-two days added onto my sentence. I don't think I'd been inside for forty-two days and there was me getting them all over again, and I hadn't even been back to court yet.

I tried arguing with the screws on the way back to the shitty cell, but it's times like that when you learn about different types of screws. All the ones down the block are bastards, well the ones at Glen Dale down the block are all bastards, put it that way. There were two massive ones who I always remember and a really fat SO, what they call the Senior Officer, who was the boss down there. One of the big ones, who was probably forty or summat, was dead muscley and had a bald head and a tan on his arms and face. When he had his shirt sleeves up you could see all his army tattoos. The other big one had grey hair cut short and was a mean and angry fuck-face, like 24/7 pissed off. He was muscley, too. The fat SO was just a fat prick who was angry as well. There were other screws down there, a couple of women ones, but I can't remember their faces properly. They were all bastards, that's all I know.

They shoved me in the cell and slammed the door and I called them wankers as they walked away. I was pissed off. Tears came in my eyes and I was cussing everything I could think of and walking up and down in the cell, turning at the door and pacing back to the window. I kept doing that for ages, probably about two hours, thinking of DD's head with blood all over it, of Crawley giving me spliff, Boo Boo, the little girl down the Trent feeding the ducks. I was crying for hours.

The muscley bald screw opened the door and was holding a tray of food. I took it and put it on the floor. I din't say thank you and he slammed the door and walked off. A minute later he came back with a cup of grey, prison tea with sugar in it. The door shut and I slumped down under the window with the food on my knee and the cup next to me. The meal was mash potato, two sausages, gravy and a lump of sponge cake. It was nowhere near a nice meal, and the tea tasted rank, but I used it to wash the food down. I din't have no choice about that unless I wanted to starve. I ate all the food and was still hungry.

I cried more and din't know how I was gonna

handle it in that cell for seven days. Being in jail is one thing, but that cell down the block was like a cell from the olden days. It was dark and stinking, with cobwebs and stains and bogeys on the walls, and puke dried on the floor, and I was sat under the window with my arms around my knees, crunched up.

20 Alone

I was lonely there and then, more than I'd ever been in all my life. I'm not bullshitting ya either. I wanted to be back home, getting on with my mum, no fights or arguments and stress. The outside world was like a country far away, or summat mad like that. What-d'-they-call-it? A million miles away: my other life was a million miles away.

As it became dark, two screws came 'round pushing a trolley with a big jug of boiling water on, some cups and bits-and-bobs like bog rolls and little plastic tubes with plastic toothbrushes in them, like the ones ya get in cop shops. They also had bars of prison soap and razor blades. They wouldn't let me have a razor because I was being monitored at first, but after a couple of days they'd probably let me have one. What they did give me was a cup of sugary, grey prison tea, a bar of soap, and a bog roll. They said I could have the toothbrush in the morning. I asked them about a mattress and covers and they said they'd be bringing them around in a minute.

I really wanted to lay down, stretch my legs and close my eyes.

'We'll give you a book an' all,' one of them said.

I asked if I could choose a book myself and they said no, they were gonna pick one for me. I'm thinking, *oh great, what stitch up are they gonna bring back*? And they brought back the bible. Dick 'eds.

One of the screws goes, 'Well, you are a left-footer aren't ya?' They both laughed.

I din't know what they were on about. Only a couple of months later I asked another girl what a left-footer was and she said it was a diss' for a catholic. The screws knew I was a catholic, because I told 'em when I first went inside, but I din't go to church or nothing like that. I believed in a higher power, but I din't know if it was a thing, like God with a beard, or just an angel, or a load of white balls floating around in space, or whatever.

I definitely din't read the fucking bible, that's for sure. I ain't got note against people who read the bible, it's just not what I needed when I was down the block. And I was gagging for a fag.

The two screws came back with a green sheet, a green crab mat, two green, itchy blankets, a pillow, a pillow case, and one of them was dragging the mankiest mattress you've ever seen. I was gutted. I din't bother saying anything because I knew they wun't change it. I dragged all the stuff into the cell and they slammed the door for the night. I started crying again because of the state of that trampy mattress. Fuck knows how many girls had pissed on it, bled on it, who knows what on it. It was a dead thin sponge mattress and it stunk like shit. The white light in the cell was so bright I could see all the stains proper close up on the mattress and covers when I was making the bed. I put the crab mat on first, and then the sheet on top of that, and the two itchy blankets on top of the sheet. Normally, on the wings, we'd get two sheets so we can sleep in between them without the itchy blankets touching the skin, but I had to either wear my clothes or put up with the itching and pubes and fuck knows what else was on them covers. Because I was down the block for days I din't know when I was getting clean clothes, so I slept naked - well, with my knickers on - and folded up my clothes and had them under my pillow. There was no way I was leaving them on that gammy floor. Plus, sleeping on them under the pillow made them flat, like ironing, which made 'em look neater.

Obviously when you're in jail, days and nights, like the memories and that lot, mix up and you can't always remember every little detail all the time, but I'll never forget that first night in that cell down the block. I slept on my back, so my face wan't touching the pillow, so the grime on the pillow wun't come through the case and get to me, and I had a sock over my eyes. The sock was to stop the sunlight waking me up early in the morning. The thing is I'd never slept on my back in my life 'til then, so I couldn't sleep properly all night. I din't move about too much so the blankets din't itch me, and I lay there thinking how fucked up my life was. It got to the point where I couldn't cry any more, my eyes must've been red raw. All I could think about was the world outside carrying on without me, not just family and mates, the whole world, all the people everywhere getting on with living, being free, doing what they want, and I was stuck in a gloomy, dirty cell when really I should've been at college or something. I shoulda been a normal teenage girl, not worrying about fighting or getting sent down or having a criminal record. There was me living with smack-rats, robbers, murderers, bullies, and suicidal cases when I would've been buzzing to have a shitty little job at KwikSave stacking Cornflakes and biscuits. Compared to the jail life, that would have been heaven. Probably that night I had three hours of messed up, scratchy sleep and I can't remember if I had a dream or not. If I did, I'm sure it would've been about being free in Nottingham; running around, laughing like a nutter, glad to be away from those smelly walls and floors.

At some daft time in the morning the same two screws from the night before opened the door and woke me up.

One of 'em went, 'Right, get up and shove all the bedding onto the landing.'

There and then I coulda burst out crying. I was so tired, and with no mattress and blankets, even fucked up ones, I din't know how I was gonna get through the whole day not being able to lay down and go to sleep. My head was already aching and my jaw was tense from not having a cigarette for hours. It took me a minute or two to get all the covers together and pull it across the dusty floor to the door. I only had on my knickers, t-shirt and socks, I din't care if they saw my legs. I was too tired and depressed to give a shit.

Once everything was out the cell, the screws

grabbed it and dragged it off to a room nearby. Just for those few seconds I stood on the landing outside the cell, wishing I could walk around and feel a tiny bit freer. I desperately wanted to walk up and down the corridor, but as soon as the screws came out of the room they told me to get back in the cell and get dressed.

I said, 'I am dressed.' They slammed the door. Wankers.

Five minutes later they came back with a trolley with some toast, a bowl of Rice Krispies and an orange. They din't give me a metal tray to hold it all on, so I held them in my hands.

'What about some milk?' I asked. 'Margarine and a spoon?'

'You'll get them when you're dressed,' one of 'em said and I knew he wan't joking.

As soon as they locked the door I got dressed and splashed water on my face. I stood next to the door waiting for the milk. A few minutes went by and I kicked the door and shouted through the side of it that I was ready for the milk. I smacked the door with the bottom of my trainer for a good minute and a couple of the other girls down there shouted to stop the noise. A screw shouted from down the corridor that if I din't stop the racket I wun't get milk. I stopped banging and went to the window to gulp air. I had a feeling they were up to summat, but you wun't believe it. The bastards never brought the milk.

I couldn't believe that they'd do that to me, to anyone, but they did.

I ate the toast dry, two slices, and I ate the orange, too. After about three hours, not long before they came round with lunch, I scooped up the Rice Krispies with a piece of orange skin and ate them as dry as you like. It was fuckeries, and the worst thing was I was dead hungry, so I din't have a choice. Each mouthful made my mouth drier and I sipped bits of water from the taps to help wash the cereal down. That's how jail gets ya.

You'll sit with your hair all messed up, you'll smoke baccy in toilet paper, you'll fight over a first class stamp, and you'll eat dry Rice Krispies 'cause the bastards won't give you any milk. You do things in prison you wouldn't do on the out.

I can't remember what they gave me for lunch, but I do know I din't say anything about the Rice Krispies and milk. I din't want them to get what-d'ya-call-it? The satisfaction: I din't want them to get the satisfaction of knowing I ate the breakfast dry and having no milk pissed me off. It's like a game, really, them versus me, and I wasn't gonna bait myself up too easy, that's for sure.

I was so knackered after lunch that I couldn't stop myself from sleeping on the hard, metal bed frame. It was like strips of metal going down length ways and then strips of metal going across width ways. Like a grid, making squares. It was solid and it dug in to my shoulders, spine, hips, and arse. I had to do it though, because I needed to go to sleep, to stop myself thinking about being locked up in a cell with nothing except a bible and my clothes. I felt like I was buried in that cell, right at the bottom of the pile of life, like the littlest piece of shit. I realised that if I din't move on the bed, if I stayed still and din't fidget, then the feeling of the metal on ma body kind of went numb and I could get some shut eye. I probably slept for a couple of hours, even though it felt like five minutes.

21 Zahra

I woke up because there was a girl kicking off in the corridor outside my cell.

I opened my eyes and jumped up to listen at the side of the door. I had my ear pressed against it. There was the sound of shoes and trainers scuffling on the floor, making a squeaking sound and there were different voices shouting all mad shit.

'Let go of the officer's arm!'

'Stop spitting you little bitch!'

The girl was screaming, 'You fucking bastards, I'll kill ya!'

There must've been five or six screws on one con.

The noise and screaming moved away to the cell on the right, next to mine. I went to the toilet and put my tab to the wall. The noise was still going on inside the next cell, the girl was screaming. I felt sorry for her, even though I din't know who it was, especially 'cause I know two or three of those screws were built like brick shit-houses and din't mess about.

It sounded like she was getting done over.

The screws pissed off and slammed the door and I could hear her sobbing and talking to herself. I banged on the wall and shouted if she was alright. She din't say anything.

I banged again and she went, 'What?'

I goes, 'Are you alright?'

She goes, 'I can't hear ya!'

I climbed up on the toilet and put my mouth near the little square air vent and asked her if she was alright.

She's like, 'No, I'm not fucking alright 'cause of those bastards!'

Then she must have ran to the door and booted it as

hard as she could because she was whacking it and screaming.

'You bastards! You fucking bastards!'

I started kicking my radiator, which is just like a whole wall of metal and makes loadsa noise when ya hit it. I was laughing as well, I'm not sure why. I suppose because we were breaking the rules.

A screw came to my door and opened it dead quick to catch me as I was about to kick the radiator again. He was angry as fuck, with a red face and fat body and hairy arms. He said if I dared do it one more time I'd be down the block for another week. I could see that he hated me. I heard the other screws wrestling with the girl next door, giving her more beats, so I thought, *fuck it*, and banged the radiator again a few times in front of the angry screw. I'd never seen him before and I'll never forget his face because it was really red, like he loved his booze too much. He walked into the cell and used his right hand to grip me by my neck and hold me against the radiator. He was squeezing my neck and had his face up in mine, so I could smell his cigarette breath. I couldn't breathe properly and started to push him away 'cause I was panicking. He used his force to fling me across the cell and I lost my feet and tripped on to the floor. I put my hands up to feel my sore neck and said, 'I'm getting you done!'

The angry screw laughed, 'Who's going to believe you, ya little slag? Now keep ya noise down!"

He walked out and locked the door.

I cried so much that snot was coming out of my nose. I curled up on the metal frame and let the tears flow.

I hated the screws. I hated the police. I hated the Judges. I hated Robert Henley. I was swearing so angry that tears were spitting off my lips.

Outside my cell the whole block was quiet. The girl next door must have been terrorized as well and the only sound I heard were keys jangling every now and then. I stayed scrunched up for ages. After a while I fell asleep thinking I was maybe gonna go mad if I was locked up down the block any longer. I needed the sleep to escape from that cell, that's all I could do. There was no other way out.

A few screws came 'round with trays of pies and mash potatoes, and because I was pissed off about being strangled and pushed over, I shut the door on 'em and said I din't want none of their fucking food. They laughed and carried on giving the tea out to whoever wanted it. I heard the girl next door getting hers because I heard her say thank-you. I wondered how she could accept anything from them after the way they'd treated her.

I walked up and down the cell, biting my nails and figuring the best way to get the screw back for grabbing me and dashing me on the ground. I din't wanna be in there, down the block or in jail, but I couldn't let them do that to me. I was a little girl to them; they're big blokes, probably with daughters of their own. How would they feel if they knew some bastard strangled their daughter? That's what I'm saying.

Nothing gave them the right to do that to me and I couldn't get the thought of the whole scene out of my head. When the screw was squeezing his fist around my throat it hurt. My eyes were popping up and all sorts. Then he's gonna go home and say goodnight to his kids and wash the pots and shag his missis, and all the while he's at work knocking girls about. He reminded me of the punter on the beat in Radford who punched me to the ground and drove off.

Cowards, that's what they are to me, they act like big men, but really they're weak bastards who pick on girls. And I'm not saying that girls can't have it with men, I'd like to see him do the same to Valerie and get away with it. I'm just saying he's abusing his power, his authority over weaker people who are locked up with no-one to look out for 'em. That's what screwed me up the most: the fact he was probably driving home laughing to himself about dashing me around and there's me crying my eyes out.

I din't have a hard enough punch or kick to do him any trouble. I could snot up a big greenie and spit it right in his face, and then he'd always have that memory of being gobbed on.

I din't bother to get up off the floor under the window when two screws shoved my bedding into the cell. I din't look at them. I waited 'til they'd gone and slowly pulled the mattress and bed pack over to the frame and made my bed.

I wanted somebody to rescue me. I know it sounds daft, especially because I caused enough of the trouble myself, but I wanted some official guy in a posh suit to burst into the shitty cell with loadsa paperwork and say there'd been a massive mistake, they were gonna let me out to do community service instead. All I had to do was sign the paperwork and I could get the fuck out of there.

After it'd been dark for a while and I'd been laid in my bed - remembering great times in the hostel like smoking draw and snorting lines of billy, or even further back than that, like at Christmas when I was ten and I got a brand new BMX that was the best present I ever got - the girl in the cell next to me banged on the wall. At first I din't move, I listened and for some reason held my breath.

She banged it again, two or three times.

I shouted, 'Go on!'

That's what everyone said. Nobody ever said, 'Yes, how may I help you?' They never said, 'What can I do for you?'

The normal thing was to say, 'Go on!'

'Go on, I'm listening!'

'Come to the vent!' She said.

'Gimme a sec'.'

I climbed out of bed and slipped my trainers on. I had my t-shirt on, the usual prison blue one, a pair of white prison knickers that probably three hundred girls had worn before me, and a pair of grey socks. I wore the socks all the time because I couldn't let my feet touch the dirty floor, especially around the toilet.

I got my creps on and walked over to the bog area and stepped up onto the back of the toilet where there was just enough space to stand with both feet flat. The vent above the toilet was a small square, like the size of a photo' or postcard, and it was close to the ceiling so I had to stretch my neck a bit and make sure my mouth was facing the holes.

I said, 'Go on,' turning my right ear toward the vent.

'What's your name?' She whispered.

I'm good at guessing where people are from, and even though she was whispering, I could tell she was from Nottingham.

'Gizmo.'

'Is that your proper name?'

'It's my nickname.'

'What's your proper name?'

'Stephanie Walters. Call me Steph' or Gizmo. What's yours?'

'Zahra.'

'Where's that name from?' It definitely sounded foreign.

'I don't know, but my dad's from Mauritius.'

I goes, 'Where in Notts' are you from?'

'How did you know I was from Nottingham?'

I could tell by her accent.

Zahra asked me where I was from.

'Meadows and Radford, mainly.'

Zahra was from Lenton.

'Did they rush you earlier?' Zahra asked.

'I was banging my radiator when you were banging your door and one of 'em came in, the one with black hair and hairy arms and hands, and he strangled me and threw me on the floor.'

'Bastard!' Zahra spat.

'What did they do to you?' Zahra said that they rushed into the cell, hit her with truncheons, and rolled her up in blankets until she calmed down. They were calling her racist names as well, threatening to rape her and hang her from the window grid and ring her mum and dad and tell 'em she committed suicide. I thought that was a horrible idea, dying in a jail cell and no-one would know you were killed by screws.

'Imagine if they did that?' Zahra asked.

22 Piss Pot

Zahra was down the block because screws had gone to her cell and told her that they had intelligence on her that she was involved in selling smack and crack in the prison.

Zahra did have five wraps of brown in her knickers, so she went along with some of the strip search, when two bitch screws asked her to take off her bra and lift up her tits, but when they said to take off her bottoms and knick-knacks she told 'em to do one because it was against her religion. Obviously she was saying that because the wraps were in her pants and she din't have time to get rid of them up her fanny or anything.

The two women screws were going, 'Take ya bottoms off now or you'll be restrained,' and Zahra kept telling them no.

Zahra was stood in her cell, in front of the window, facing the two screws and they had their backs to the door. Outside a couple of bloke screws were waiting for the strip-search to happen so they could go in and search the cell. There was a security screw with a smelly little sniffer-dog as well, which all the girls hated going in their cells because its hair got everywhere, plus it stank like they never washed it. Zahra knew she would be in serious trouble if they found the wraps, so she slid her left hand inside her knickers at exactly the same time as she swung her right arm 'round and slapped the screw to her left in the face as hard as she could. The screw screamed and fell back against the sink. Zahra looked at the other screw, a skinny woman fresh out of screw school, looking bummy and reaching for her truncheon, and went to back-hand her as she dropped the wraps of gear in to the bog. The wraps hit the water. Zahra's back-hand din't connect because the skinny screw grabbed her arm with one hand and held up the truncheon and told Zahra to stay still, but Zahra needed to flush the toilet, and she had hardly any time to do it because the screw she'd already slapped grabbed her left arm, so she was being held by both of 'em. The men screws were starting to rush the cell too.

It looked like Zahra was fucked, they definitely woulda found the wraps floating in the toilet as soon as they cleared the cell and searched it properly, so she forced the women screws backwards into the path of the two bloke screws, dipped her head forward, and slammed her forehead against the cheek of the screw she'd already slapped. The woman fell back, letting go of Zahra's arm, so Zahra pressed the flush button on the bog, just as the other woman screw started hitting her shoulders and back with the solid black truncheon. The male screws started moving to dive on her and bring her to the floor. When they realised the bog was flushing, one of the men stuck his arm into the grimey water to try and grab the small package before it was sucked into the sewers, but it was too late, the smack had gone through the pipes.

Zahra said she nearly went unconcious from the beats they were giving her after the drugs disappeared but she was glad they din't have the evidence. They dragged her to the block and that's when I first heard her shouting and getting more digs.

Zahra said, 'The one that strangled you punched me in my tits and ribs, he's a bastard.'

That's when I thought, *I'm gonna get that fucker!*

I din't tell Zahra about my plan, I don't know why, she probably would've thought I was just bigging myself up. We carried on chatting about how fuckeries the screws were and Zahra asked me if I smoked and I was like, 'Yeah, but I ain't 'ad a fag for two days!'

Zahra was like, 'Send me a line and I'll send ya a couple of burns and some matches yeah?'

Zahra already had tobacco, Rizla, and matches because one of the other girls down there had shoved them under her door on the way to the shower. Zahra knew enough girls in Glen Dale, so even down the block she was getting sorted out.

When you sell drugs inside you can get everything you need to live lively and comfortable as well as make cash. You need links on the out to make proper dosh though, otherwise you end up with toiletries, tobacco, and phone cards and not much else. Still, it's good to make a raise in jail anyway you can. If you can trust people on the out then you get the jail fiends to send money from their prison accounts to them, and your connection cashes the postal orders and saves the loot for you and sends you some when you need it. That's how organised jail dealers work. Plus the fiends can get their mates or family to drop cash off at the dealer's link's house or on a street corner. Then the dealer will ring their people to make sure the money's dropped off, and if it is then they'll sort the drugs out on the wing. It's a bit trickier to run your game like that because you need a mobile on the inside to chat properly, otherwise everyone would have to wait longer to arrange shit on their visits.

To send a line to Zahra, I had to pull pieces of the itchy bitchy blankets out and tie the ends together to make a long bit of string. Every prisoner in the country has heard of throwing lines because it's one of the main ways of passing stuff about when you're locked behind your door.

I had my long piece of string all tied so that it wun't snap easy, I ripped a chunk of the cover off the bible, like a nice square bit of it, and wrapped one end of my line around it and tied it so it stayed on. I shouted Zahra and asked her if she was ready with her line and she was. I slid the piece of bible dead fast under my door using all my power, towards Zahra's cell next door. The first couple of times my line din't go near her door. Eventually it bounced off the opposite wall and stopped right near it. Zahra slid her line out, which had a bit of broken-off plastic knife tied on, and as she pulled it in slowly it caught on mine and dragged it in as well. Zahra stuck two rolled burns on it, two matches, and a bit of strike off a matchbox, and I pulled it in, under my door.

I was buzzing to have a fag after all the hours of not having one, and the first few drags went to my head and I got a little numb feeling in my face and arms and tits an' that, a proper nicotine rush.

I shouted, 'Respect!'

Zahra replied, 'Safe,' and that she was getting her head down. I smoked one of the burns standing at the window, blowing the smoke through the holes in the grid. I was still thinking of what the screw did to me earlier in the day, but I was buzzing I'd got chatting to Zahra, because it took some of the boredom and loneliness away. Before I got back in bed to try and fall asleep, I took my blue plastic cup to the toilet area and squatted over the smelly bog and started to do a piss, and just as I was finishing I held the cup under my fanny and filled it up with wee. I put it next to the wall near the door, so if it was opened the screws couldn't see it, then I got back in bed and lay there smiling about what I was gonna do with the cup of piss. I was thinking about it so much I couldn't sleep for ages and lay in bed getting nervous, but the main thing in my head was whether the screw that strangled me was gonna be working in the block the next day or not.

I must have fell asleep about three in the morning or summat. I was so knackered that I only woke up as the lock in the cell door cracked open and a screw stepped in the pad and shouted something stupid like, 'Walters! Get up for breakfast!' I lifted my head from under the covers and saw that it was a black man screw who I'd never seen before. I said I din't want breakfast, even though I was hungry, I just wanted to sleep, but he said I had to get up to put the mattress and bed stuff outside the cell. My eyes felt like they were glued together, I was so tired, and it took me a few extra minutes to get the shit together.

The black screw walked away to open Zahra's door to get her mattress, covers, and sheets. As I got to my door to shove everything out onto the corridor I noticed the other screw stood with the trolley of breakfasts. My heart started thumping like mad. It was the screw who strangled me and hit Zahra the day before. He looked at me and smiled a little bit and said something like, 'Have you calmed down now then, Walters?' He was talking like he din't want no stress.

I said 'Yeah, I suppose so.' Maybe he felt guilty about what he did to us and he wanted to be sweet with me, but I wan't watching that. I wan't in the mood for forgiveness.

In case he shut the door on me before I could get the cup, I started to reach down behind the opened door and say, 'Boss, can you tell me what this is, please.' I made my voice sound soft, grabbed the cup and stood up straight.

The dick head screw said, 'What?' He leaned into the cell just as I stood in front of him.

Then I goes, 'This, you bastard,' and flicked the yellow piss right in his face, and then slammed the door as he put his hands up to his wet head and shouted the other screws to come.

My blood was pumping faster around my veins and I clenched my fists and went and stood in front of the window, facing the closed door. I heard keys jingle and footsteps running and I was scared.

I could hear Zahra at the vent shouting, 'What's happened?' I din't say anything back to her.

The keys and the running stopped and I heard screws talking in low tones.

I screamed, 'Come on then, you wankers! Come and strangle me again!' My veins must've been bulging out of my head and neck, that's how hyped up I was, I'm tellin ya.

The lock on the cell door clicked and the observation flap opened and there were three sets of angry eyes watching me. I was bummy as fuck, but there was no escape. I stood hoping that whatever they were going to do was gonna be over quickly.

23 Bastards

The door opened wide and three screws walked into the cell with their truncheons out. It was the black guy, a white, fat senior officer with a massive beer belly, and a young looking screw with a tanned face, black hair like Superman, and tattoos on his arms. All of them looked angry and were saying stuff like, 'You little bitch!'

'You're never getting out of here!'

'You're gonna wish you din't do that!'

They crept towards me. The black screw was dead muscley and his arms were all bulging and his eyes looked like they were gonna burst. He stepped closer than the other two and got dead near with his truncheon raised up above his head.

'Get on your knees!' He said, with proper tensed teeth and I knew he wan't going to tell me again.

I slowly got on my knees. I kept looking in his eyes, in case he was gonna whack me when I looked away.

His teeth were still clenched. 'Now put your hands behind your back!'

'What you gonna do to me?' I said, obviously frightened.

The fat SO stepped closer.

'Just fucking do as he tells you!'

I put my hands behind my back. The young black-haired screw came behind me and got down, and I could tell he was fidgeting with keys and whatever, and then he grabbed my wrist and put a pair of handcuffs on me. He put 'em on tight an' all and I asked if they could be loosened.

'You'll get fuck all!' The SO said.

The black screw stepped backwards and the young screw said, 'Up!' He pulled me up by my arms and as I got to my feet the young screw moved away and the SO stepped to me and whacked me across my right thigh with his truncheon so hard that I had white flashes in my eyes and I dropped and started crying. The pain was deadly, I swear. I could hear other girls shouting to leave me alone and someone was kicking her door. It was probably Zahra.

The SO brought the truncheon down on me again, this time on my left leg, and the pain went straight through me like being shot or summat like that. I screamed like mad and said 'I'm sorry, I'm sorry, I'm sorry.' Deep down I wasn't sorry, I din't wanna get hit like that no more. Even if you hit a big bloke like that, it would hurt. The blow on my left leg made me lift my knees up and lean back onto my handcuffed hands.

I begged them not to hit me again and they laughed and walked out of the cell saying stuff like, 'Not so hard now are ya?' They giggled like teenage bullies. I had tears running down my face, but I had to get up to take the pressure off my hands. My legs were throbbing with pain and my wrists must've been nearly bleeding. I stood still with my bum against the wall at the end of the bed frame and dropped my head and watched the tears land with splashes on the dirty cell floor.

Zahra banged on the wall and asked if I was ok. I shouted like she did the day before.

'The fucking bastards have handcuffed me and whacked me!'

The cell door opened again and I stood up in pain, tears dripping from my cheeks. Four screws came in. The black one, the short fat SO, the black-haired young one, and the one I chucked piss over. They walked right inside the cell and pushed the door nearly shut. With tears and spit falling off my chin, arms handcuffed behind my back, and my hair all over the place, I must've looked a mess. The one who I threw piss over looked weird because he still had his black trousers and boots on, but he was wearing a large, blue prison t-shirt as well. The piss must've gone on his shirt, he needed summat clean to wear. He half looked like a prisoner, and just as pissed off as one. The black screw and the fat SO had their weapons out, above their heads. The young one stepped to me and took the handcuffs off, I din't say note, but I kept clocking the one I chucked piss on 'cause I expected him to punch me. They all came closer and I cried louder, cuz I ain't gonna lie to ya, I was scared, and the way they moved it was obvious they were on a mission.

The one I threw piss on grabbed me by my shoulders and I started screaming, the young one grabbed me as well and they slammed me down on to the bed frame and the pain in my legs got worse, plus I was winded by dropping onto the metal on my back. The black one and the fat SO grabbed my legs, they must've put their tools down 'cause they had both hands on me, and they started pulling at my knickers and I was still shouting, 'Please don't, get off me, I'm sorry,' and stuff like that. The young one shoved summat like a flannel or summat over my mouth and he told me to stop making noise, it would only make things worse. They pulled my knickers off and had my legs spread and the one I chucked piss on was going, 'Now I'm gonna fuck you, ya little slag!' I started going mad and kicking my legs and tryna get 'em away from me with my hands.

I fought with all my strength and managed to fall onto the floor on my back and I was thrashing about and calling for help. I don't know who I was expecting to come and help, but I still shouted it. Other girls, especially Zahra, were making noises and shouting and kicking their doors. One of the screws, I'm not sure which one, started slapping me in the face dead hard with his palm, and the young screw was tryna get the handcuffs back on me, and I was tryna hide my face and pull my arms free. Next thing I knew the black officer is sitting on my legs with all his power and weight and the fat SO got his hefty knee digging right in my chest. My hands were cuffed and the young one got the cloth or whatever it was over my mouth and I'm still tryna make a noise. I was wriggling a little bit, but I had pain all over my body: my face from the slaps, my back from being winded, my legs from the truncheons, and my chest from the fucking fat SO digging his fat knee into me. I looked up and the screw I lobbed wee on had his little sausage cock out of his zip and - just as piss started to splurt out - the young screw moved the cloth away from my gob and I shouted summat, but piss landed on my face. I started screaming again, piss was going in my eyes, up my nose, even in my mouth I admit, it was going in my mouth and splashing everywhere. For about five seconds he pissed on me and I couldn't do anything about it.

He put his dick away and laughed, 'That'll show you wont it, eh?'

One of 'em undid the handcuffs. I rolled onto my belly and put my hands up to wipe the waz off my face. The taste was horrible, like salty tea or summat. I was crying like a baby does when it's sobbing so much it starts shaking its whole body and hiccuping. That was me, wobbling and shaking. I was in bits, put it that way. I looked around for my knickers and they were under the bed frame. I slipped 'em on and went to the sink and splashed water on my face and neck. I did it loads, till I thought all the wee was washed off my skin. I looked at my thighs and the bruises started coming up even worse, on each leg they went from my hips right down to my kneecaps and they were spread all 'round the thigh except the back bit. You wun't think two whacks would bruise you like that, but it does, believe me. Big, blue, and dead sore bruises, that's what they were. My lips were sore from the slaps and my wrists had blisters from the handcuffs.

I started walking up and down, still crying. I was wondering how I was gonna get out of the block without going mad.

24 Pain

Each time I moved my legs to walk, the big muscles in my thighs made the bruises feel like they were being poked, so I started to shuffle around the pad slowly because of the pain. I din't have no breakfast, but I did still have a roll-up that I'd saved from the night before. I got it from the window sill and lit it with my last match. I still had tears in my eyes.

Zahra banged on the wall and shouted me to come to the vent. My legs were so painful that I couldn't even climb the back of the bog and I called to Zahra from the window instead.

'What the fuck happened, babes?' She asked.

My voice was shakey from the stress and the crying and I din't really wanna speak.

'They whacked me with the truncheons.'

'Why, what did ya do?'

'I chucked a cup of piss on one of 'em.'

'Did ya?' Zahra was buzzing, saying I was a rude-girl and she shouted the other girls down there and told 'em. They were buzzing and calling out to me and saying what I did was wicked and that the screw deserved it.

I din't bother shouting back. I wanted to enjoy my fag, it was the only luxury I had and I wan't sure when I was gonna get any other treats. I din't wanna talk to anyone and I was so messed up, I probably would've just started crying if I chatted loads. I blew smoke out the window and watched it floating off. I felt like I'd been ran over, but the worse thing was there was nobody around who gave a shit.

I had a random memory of a time when me, my mum, and Sebella went to Skegness for a few days and we ran out of sun-cream. Me and Sebella got sun-burn and had to cotch in the tent with soaking wet t-shirts on our backs and shoulders. My mum watched over us, from outside the tent, feeling guilty because she din't have any money to get any cream or food, or even tickets for the train back to Notts', but she had one last roll up. She was waiting for ages to smoke it, like she was saving it for a special moment, like it was the last fag my mum was ever gonna have. I was on my belly in the tent, with the damp t-shirt on my back getting warm because of the heat from the red sun-burn, and I was watching my mum light the last roll up. She was sitting cross-legged, facing me. I had my hand over my eyes to stop the sun shining in 'em and my mum goes, 'It's not the last one forever, eh Steph'?'

I was like, 'No ma, it's not the last one forever.'

When I was stood at the block cell window I was saying that to myself.

'It's not the last one forever, Gizmo.' I finally knew what it meant: hope.

I took one last drag on the burn and flicked the nub onto the overgrown grass outside the cell window. No prisoners went gardening there, I tell ya that. There were crisp packets and fag nubs and other rubbish. Probably no-one had been on that grass since the prison was first built; weeds up to ya knees and cobwebs and insects all growing and living like it was their own little universe. Only the poor bastards that spent time down the block in Glen Dale saw it, and we chucked our rubbish into it to add to the mess. It was the only bit of greenery that I saw when I was in jail, and even though people had fucked it up, it was still satisfying to see some nature and the breeze blowing the grass.

It's crazy, all the stuff you appreciate after you've been banged up. I'm not just on about drugs, or shocking out in the jungle tent of the carnival, or chilling with a big spliff after a nice dinner, or having an ice-cream out and about, watching in the Arbo' when all the heads are lazing around and no-one's stressing about going on a raise. I'm talking about watching birds that you don't even know the name of flying about the sky. I'm on about missing the rain on ya face, or that tingly feeling ya get when ya walking on fresh cut grass with no creps or socks on. It was thinking like that that made me start feeling wounded about being a prisoner.

I started getting bummy thinking I was gonna get a big sentence. I can't even describe it properly, but it's like the way you get when you think you've seen a ghost or the way you get scared when you choke on a piece of apple for ten seconds. It's like that, but it stays with you for a full day or a whole night. As soon as I started thinking of what bird the Judge was gonna give me, the scared vibe would lock in and I couldn't eat or concentrate. None of the girls chatted about it because nobody wanted to look like they couldn't hack it or whatever, but I reckon all prisoners get the panic.

Two days after my beating, when I'd been down the block for a few days in that disgusting cell, they came and told me I was going back to a normal wing, what they call 'general population'.

I wasn't nicked for the piss-pot over the screw and I din't have to serve the full seven days that the Governor sentenced me to. I din't ask why: I din't care, I was glad to be out of there.

For a couple of days before I went I spoke loads to Zahra at the vent and we kept each other company for hours. We became good mates, we had a laugh, and she saved me twos on every burn she was given by other girls.

The maddest thing was we never saw each other face to face, and we never spoke again. Never. Even if Zahra walked past me in the street tomorrow, I wun't recognise her, but we made a connection. We battled our corner. I probably woulda done a lot more crying and screaming if I'd been down the block on my own. I heard that Zahra had to do a couple of months down there, because they suspected she was getting drugs smuggled in - which she was - and then they shipped her out to a jail miles away up north. Good luck to her, anyway, wherever she ended up.

I went back on the unit I was on before, in the same cell. Di had moved to a single pad near Crawley on the three's landing, and a small black girl called Shanice was my new cell mate. She was from Leicester, in for robbery on some girl outside a club. She had a pretty face, tiny hands and feet. I don't know how she robbed anyone, 'cause she was so small, but that's what she was in for. Shanice had quite long hair, in the relaxed style that loads of black girls have, and she was fretting that the jail shop wun't have the proper creams and shampoos for it and her skin as well. She was seventeen like me, with a squeaky voice, and she was in a gang from the rough area in Leicester called Highfields. She tidied the cell, and now all my shampoos and deodorants and that lot were all cleaned and neat in a row on the table against the wall. Shanice din't really have much stuff because she'd only been in for a couple of days. I'd left teabags, stamps, paper and pens, biscuits, and a few other bits-and-bobs from before I was down the block and Shanice hadn't touched any of 'em. I respected her for that because she coulda used 'em and blamed someone else, or she coulda sold 'em and told me the screws took everything, but she cleaned the pad and left my shit alone, so when I walked back into the cell and saw it was all cool I was buzzing and we got on straight away.

Shanice had nabbed the top bunk, where I liked to sleep, but I din't care too tough about it then because I was so happy to be out the block and laid down on a normal mattress in a fresh cell. It was like getting out of the police station after a couple of days and going home, a mini-freedom or summat.

Me and Shanice were chatting about what music we liked and the dances we could do, even though I'm a shit dancer, and just chatting like that while I was trying to relax my bruised legs on the bed, and Crawley came to the door and smiled through the flap. I was excited to see Crawley, plus I wanted Shanice to see that I had mates and knew people on the wing.

Crawley was all smiling an' buzzing.

'Alright?'

'Yeah, of course. Look at these thighs.' I pulled

down my tracksuit bottoms to show my bruised thighs.

'Was that for throwing the piss?' Crawley asked.

'Ow did ya know about that?'

'Every fucker knows about that! You're famous kidder!' Crawley was happy that I'd come back.

'Who told you?' I asked, shocked that the whole jail knew about it.

'The block orderly, she told everyone down gym, said piss went in his mouth and everything!'

The block orderly is the prisoner that works for the screws down the block, mopping and cleaning and making cups of tea. I din't even see her the whole time I was down there.

All I could think of was that everyone was chatting about me and bigging me up. I messed DD up and chucked piss on a screw, so people musta been thinking, *this girl's crazy* and rating me.

Crawley asked what happened and I told her the whole story, from when I heard them hitting Zahra to them beating me. I never told her that I got pissed on. That woulda been a bait and brought shame on my name, everyone woulda just laughed and thought I was a muppet.

Crawley goes, 'Wankers, aren't they?'

I'm like, 'Yeah, course. At least I'm back now though, eh?'

Crawley pointed her finger down, made a sign to be quiet and bent to push a bit of tissue under the door. I grabbed and opened the tissue. It was a little chunk of hash and a blue tablet.

I was made up.

'Thanks mate!'

I wrapped the drugs up and shoved 'em in my sock. Shanice asked what it was and I said I'd show her in a minute.

Crawley put her mouth up to the hinge of the door.

'Blaze that later, after bang up and the blue thing's a diazepam. It will knock you out.' Crawley leaned back and smiled at me through the flap window.

I held my thumb up to say thanks and she did summat I'll never forget. Crawley kissed her fingers and pressed them against the glass, smiled and said, 'I'll see you later.'

25 My Pad

I span around to see if Shanice saw what Crawley did. She was looking out the window, so she couldn't have. My heart was all over the place and my mouth was dry, like I was dead nervous all of a sudden.

Di and a couple of others came to the door and I told the story of what happened and showed them my bruises. They were offering me baccy and shampoos, stamps and magazines to read. That was all good. I din't think of it at first, not from Di anyway, cause I saw her as a mate already, but the rest of them wanted to be my mate. Shanice said they were, 'Begging friend'.

I was on my bed thinking about it. I got back from the shitty block and there were enough girls coming to check me, Crawley linking me with drugs for free, Di bringing her smiles and her mates and their cronies begging friendship from me and giving me stuff. It felt great, but I din't wanna start shouting off about it or anything. I din't want Shanice to think I had a big head. At the end of the day, I wanted Shanice to like me and not disrespect me. I probably could have battered her anyway, I just din't want trouble. She was in a gang of girls in Leicester connected to a gang of lads, so people called her a rude-girl: some people thought I was a rude-girl as well. We'd done some of the same things in life, like robbing and getting in trouble, and we were both street wise, and I wan't scared of her or anything. I actually liked her, but I kind of got this vibe from her that she din't really like white people. She told me of times white people, men and women and kids, had been racist to her when she was growing up. I mean, I thought that was bad, obviously, 'cause I was brought up to not be racist. I felt funny about Shanice going on about white people the way she did, because there's me, a white girl, and I'm not racist an' I was feeling like she's getting on at me like it's my fault. I told her that all my family history, what's-it-called? Ancestral. My ancestral history was from Ireland and I was only called Walters because it changed from O'Rourke somewhere down the line when one of my Grandmas got married. I told Shanice that Irish people through history had been abused and fucked up by England. She din't really know anything about it, and I only knew some of it, but I could tell she din't think the racism and the slave trade in her ancestral history were the same as the racism, slavery, potato famine, and what-not in mine. I told her Irish and other white people like gypsies and criminals and nutcases had been on some slave ships and she wan't sure about that. Boo Boo Girl told me that. We din't argue about it, I just tried to hold my corner and explain that I felt bad about shit from history and that I grew up in a rough manor and got trouble from the police because of where I lived and things like that.

Shanice was into dancing and she could sing as well. Shanice was small and compact, with small legs, and when she danced around the pad she looked proper, like she was born to dance. She had great moves. I loved watching her, and she could sing that Shola Ama song *You Might Need Somebody* perfect. I used to ask her to sing that all the time, and when she did she belted it out and I clapped along and Shanice done a few moves to it an' all. It was sweet.

I showed Shanice the draw and diazepam tablet after lunch, when there were no screws around, and she said I shun't take the tablet because it was for druggies and smack-heads. Shanice din't know that I took near enough any drug except for smack and crack I could get my hands on. I din't want her to start dissing me, so I said I would sell it later on association.

I was looking forward to going on association that night because all the girls on the wing would see me and I'd be able to check out what they were saying about me.

I was wondering what Crawley was on with when she blew me a kiss through the glass in my door. I definitely liked her, although I was a bit scared. I snogged girls before, in school and that, and I even let Nicola Hall rub me up in her dad's garage one time. Me and Nicola used to snog lots and touch each other and whatever, but until I'd met Crawley I'd not done ote proper with another girl or woman. I knew I liked other girls, and I knew I fancied boys as well, and that's bisexual. I class myself as bi, but I don't broadcast it to people when I meet them. When I thought about Crawley, like picturing her in the showers naked next to me, I fantasised about kissing her and touching her and licking her tattoos and crazy shit like that. I din't know loads about lesbian sex, I just thought it was fingering each other and snogging and that. I know more now, but then I din't know shit, really. I was thinking, *I bet Crawley knows all about it.* She looked like she knew, put it that way. Crawley was like a taller, sexier, and smarter version of Valerie. I din't think of Valerie in a fancying way, though. She was too tom-boy for me, but Crawley kept herself looking feminine and I liked that a lot. She had a tan all over her body, making her look like she was Spanish or summat. I think she might have had foreign blood in her, I cant remember if she mentioned it. Up close she was still pretty and she din't need makeup to look attractive, which is not the usual way for most girls. Crawley could still look hard and serious, it's just she din't look like a bloke or lad when she was. If you saw her shopping in town, and you couldn't see her tattoos, and you din't hear her speaking slang or ote, then you'd think she was a good looking straight women, but when you looked at Val, you knew she was a tom-boy, well, I did anyway. That's why I started to fancy Crawley: she wan't scary like Valerie could be.

I went on association: loads of girls were looking at me and nodding towards me like they were on about what I'd been doing. I stood near the pool table because Crawley was playing. I wan't gonna play, I din't do pool. Girls would get smacked up over who was next to play and shit like that. One time I saw a girl's jaw get broken 'cause she got a pool cue wrapped around her head for running her mouth off over a game. I'm talking two of her teeth popped out, blood everywhere. It ain't worth it and it ain't an' interesting game anyway. I stood watching Crawley lose. She came off the table and we gave each other a hug. Girls are always hugging each other in prison. I suppose it's like blokes shaking hands or respecting each other with their fists together.

Crawley spoke as we squeezed each other.

'I'm glad you're out the block, it's getting boring here.'

I was like, 'I don't know what I can do to change that, mate.'

She goes, 'Well, you can keep me company, can't ya?'

'What shall we do then?'

Crawley pulled a spliff from the sleeve of her prison tracksuit and showed it me before anyone else saw it, quickly hiding it away after I'd clocked it.

'Lets go and blaze this in the bogs, yeah?'

We walked off to the bogs, which were away from the screws and near the showers where the back doors of the wing and the rubbish bins were.

A few girls were in the bogs doing dodgy dealings and when Crawley sparked up the spliff one of 'em begged for twos, and then another one for threes.

'She's got twos,' Crawley said, pointing at me.

We went into a cubicle under the open window and locked the door. One of the girls was like, 'Please Crawley, don't be like that!'

Crawley goes, 'Fuck off, get your own. Stop baiting me up and saying my name!'

'Is it like that then?' The girl asked.

'Yeah, it's like that,' Crawley said, 'now piss off!'

The spliff was packed full of hash and the smoke was dead thick. One or two drags was enough to start feeling red. On the out I was used to toking all the time and skunk weed as well, not just hash, but after five or six weeks or whatever it was, without regular draw, one spliff would knock my head off. I swear, when I was stood in that cubicle

I could feel the vibe already. My whole head was tingling and my heart was beating faster 'cause we could have been caught by a screw. We were blowing the smoke out the window, but a screw could do a normal check on the bogs any time they wanted. Most of the times I smoked weed in prison I got paranoid because I'd be looking at the screws and the girls that were grasses and thinking, *they know I'm red, they can see it in my eyes.* Even if they din't have a fucking clue what I'd been up to, I still thought they'd know just from the way they looked at me. When ya first go inside its okay to smoke and get caught, because you can't get done 'cause it takes about twenty eight days for ganja to come out your body completely. If you go in jail and blaze for the first few weeks you'd be alright, 'cause you can just say you were smoking right up to the day you got arrested, it's still in your system from then. I'd been in over a month, I din't have an excuse and a guilty on a piss test, like a positive on a test by the scientists or whatever, could get you twenty-one extra days on ya sentence. Girls drank loads of orange juice and water to get rid of the drugs in their bodies and sometimes that was enough to beat the tests. It made you wee loads, but it was worth it.

A way to stop screws and grasses from smelling it coming from a cell was to tip a load of talcum powder on to a towel and flap the towel around the cell, like when your getting dust from a rug, and the talc goes everywhere, but kind of disappears for a bit and makes the pad smell nice. We used to rub shampoo and shower gel on the radiators when they were warm and that used to give off a clean smell around the pad, too. The only thing with the talcum powder mission was that you'd get a thin layer of talc on your floor by the morning, and if the screws who knew the score saw it they'd come back and search your cell and send you for a piss test. To make sure they din't see it we used to get up as early as we could to wipe the floor clean. Trust me, we had to do loads of shit to cover our tracks when we took drugs in prison. Most of the time it worked.

26 Sex

After me and Crawley burnt the spliff of hash in the bogs, we went upstairs to Crawley's cell to chill out.

Crawley's cell was so clean and organized I used to love being in there. I sat on the bed and watched her open one of the cupboards and pull out a pack of Maryland cookies. She offered me one and even though I knew my mouth would go dry with a biscuit, I took one out and said thanks. I crammed it in my mouth to get it out the way. I should have said, *no ta,* but I was tryna go with the flow.

I could feel the ganja buzz coming on strong, a warm glow in my head. I asked Crawley if my eyes looked red and she said they looked normal.

Crawley was moving around a bit, like pottering about, using bits of tissue to wipe the sides to get rid of the dust, adjusting her rug and photos and keeping herself busy. I enjoyed watching her.

'Shall I put some tunes on?' Crawley asked.

'If ya want.'

Crawley reached under the bed and pulled out her CD player, put it on the bed and grabbed some CD's from the cupboards.

'Stick one on.'

I flicked through the CD's as Crawley grabbed six R20 batteries from under her pillow. In jail you have to hide your property, what they call 'prop', in different places because girls will raid ya cell and nick ya stuff and think nothing about it. Stashing ya bits-and-bobs here, there and everywhere, made it harder to find it in a small time because pad thieves would rob ya cell in fifteen seconds flat. If ya prize possessions aren't out the way then they're gone. It's sad, but that's the way it is.

I picked out a heavy metal album, I think it was

Guns and Roses, and stuck it on.

'I thought you were into hip hop?' Crawley said.

'I like all sorts.'

The rock blasted and I was tapping my foot and watching Crawley clean up and wondering if she was nervous or summat because she couldn't sit down. The Sun was blazing and I looked out and saw the orange glow on the prison fence. I wished we could have been somewhere different, like on the embankment next to the Trent with a can of beer or even on holiday in Skegness or Blackpool.

I said something like, 'It's nice out there innit?'

Crawley din't hear me. I thought she might not want me in her pad, like she wanted her own space because she liked being stoned on her own. I was probably a bit paranoid.

By the time Crawley did cotch next to me, I was red, like as if I'd just smoked a five pound draw to myself. Everything looked clearer, I could see stuff better, and because it was sunny outside the cell was bright and warm.

Crawley baited it up a bit and nearly fucked up my vibe.

'You're in court next week aren't ya?'

I couldn't believe she mentioned it like that, popping my red vibe like a bubble. It's like when you take acid and your mate says something dark or moody and it gets in your head, starts to bring you down or wreck your head. That's what it is, a head-wreck. I'm not saying that's what Crawley did, but she was close, trust me. A girl can be my mate, a guy or whoever, but they can still say things that annoy me or do my head in. The last thing I wanted to think about when I was enjoying the ganja vibe was the sentence I was looking and how long left I had to ride before I could be free.

I looked out the window again.

'I'm up on Monday.'

'For sentence?'

'Yep.' I wanted to say, *don't talk about court, talk good*

times instead.

'What do you think you'll get?' Crawley asked. I suppose she cared, or she was making me think she cared.

'Fuck knows, probably six or seven years, summat like that.'

Six or seven years was the worst, that's what my solicitor said. I was so used to telling people six or seven that the years became normal to say. Seven years would have meant getting out when I was twenty-four. There and then that was a fucking lifetime away and I couldn't even get my head around having to serve years in prison. That's a long time when you're basically a kid, like I was and most of the other girls were.

'Hopefully the Judge will get his dick sucked the night before, eh?' I joked.

Crawley laughed. Prisoners always said that about sentencing and trial Judges. If the Judge got his end away then he might not give such a big sentence.

Most Judges are pricks. I read enough stories in the papers about Judges being done for noncing and child porn. I heard from other working girls that some big name Judges went to prostitutes and rent boys and took crack. Then they're sitting there on Monday morning, slamming everyone and dishing out big birds, and if they're a nonce case then they'll let the nonces off with small sentences. They're supposed to be high and mighty, but some of 'em are as bad as the crims they're sending down all day long, so the joke in jail is: all you can hope is that the Judge gets his end away the night before.

Even though we were going on about court and sentences and all that, I was still buzzin' to be with Crawley. It made me extra warm inside when I was next to her, I got the tickly feeling in my stomach and on my arms like when I was next to Mrs Melton in school. That's how I could tell for sure that I fancied Crawley. I wanted to kiss her, but I was bummy to make the first move. I thought she fancied me too, but she might not have done, and she coulda smacked me if I tried it on. Just because she blew me a kiss din't mean she was in love with me or anything. Lots of girls are like that with each other and it din't mean they wanted to get it on.

I kept moving my head slowly round to clock the door, feeling a bit dodgy like I was expecting another girl or a screw to open the door and go, *what you two doing?* I was nervous, but tryna act cool. I din't want Crawley to think I couldn't handle it.

Crawley went, 'I like you, ya know!'

I couldn't think of what to say, I couldn't look at her properly in the eyes.

'What do ya mean?' I says. I know what she meant, but I din't know what else to say.

'I fancy ya.' Crawley said.

Before I even knew what I was on about, I goes, 'I fancy you an' all.'

Crawley sat on the bed, our legs were touching.

'Can I kiss you?'

With a croak in my voice I said yes.

Crawley touched my left cheek with her right hand and leaned forward, and I closed my eyes and our lips came together. Gently her tongue poked into my mouth and I touched its softness with my own. I could taste the leftovers of the hash spliff.

Crawley pulled away and got up, 'Wait a sec,' she said and walked over to the door, pushing it shut so that we were locked in.

My heart was still going mad. Crawley grabbed a roll of toilet roll and tore a few sheets off and used her spit to stick them over the glass on the door. No-one could watch us. She pulled her t-shirt off in one go, dead quick. I felt so turned on looking at her nipples.

'Kiss them.' Crawley said, standing in front of me.

For a couple of minutes, I did as she told me. Crawley climbed onto the bed slowly, lay down on her back, and opened her legs wide.

'Kiss me 'round here.' She said, looking in my eyes and touching her fanny.

'Put your fingers in me.'

She was moaning all the while and looking down at my fingers.

Five minutes must have gone before she moaned, 'I'm gonna cum. Keep going!'

Crawley was almost screaming the pad down. 'Don't stop!'

Eventually she calmed down and whispered, 'You better wash your hand.' We both smiled and I pecked her lips and got up.

I wanted to jump around dancing, that's how happy I was. I wanted to do it again. I wanted to get naked properly and let her do it to me. I wanted to shake and cum like Crawley did.

I cleaned my hands and for some reason splashed warm water on my face, by the time I turned 'round, Crawley was putting her knickers back on. She smiled at me as she got dressed and I stood against the sink and goes, 'What shall we do now?'

I was thinking I wanted her to do it to me, but she went, 'I'm gonna go have a shower.'

I'm like, 'Oh, right.' I was still smiling, but I was feeling bait.

Crawley pressed the emergency cell bell next to the light switch.

'When a screw comes, I'll say some daft bitch locked the door on us for a joke yeah?'

'Safe,' I said, feeling like I did when I'd just been done by a punter.

Standing there confused, I heard a screw coming up the landing, his keys swinging and Crawley kissed me once on the lips and goes, 'You're special, you are.'

The screw opened the cell door and asked what was going on. We said we got locked in and he walked away, not giving a shit.

Crawley grabbed her towel and shower gel.

'I'll see you in a bit then?'

'Alright,' I said.

'I'll come and say good night to ya.'

'Alright.'

We left the cell and she walked off without looking back. I felt like shouting down the landing, *'old on a sec. Where's my fucking finger fuck?* I din't say ote: I watched her walk off the landing and I went to my own cell and cotched on my bed.

27 Used

I felt weird.

I couldn't believe I'd just properly got off with another girl, kissing her and licking her and all that, and wallop! Crawley buggers off like she's dissing me and I'm thinking I don't know what's going on. We din't have much time left on association, so I was thinking maybe Crawley went for a shower because she wun't have had enough time to do anything to me. She couldn't have just baited me up like that for no reason. I'd expected that kind of shit from a lad: fuck ya and leave ya. I thought a girl would be different. Maybe she was embarrassed. She couldn't handle it, so she mizzed out.

By the time Shanice came back to the cell at the end of association, I was all over the place about Crawley and what was gonna happen between us. I was on one, worrying she wan't even gonna chat to me again, or even look at me.

I din't say ote to Shanice about it. She would've cussed me for getting off with a girl and we probably woulda ended up fighting.

Crawley never came to say goodnight. I was feeling used, so I cotched on the bed and blazed half a spliff without blowing the smoke out of the window. I din't give a shit if the screws were gonna rush the cell and search it, they couldn't have done worse to me then what they already did. Shanice din't care either, but she did still make an effort with talcum powder and deodorant on the door and radiator.

I wanted to be stoned like I used to get on the out, not worrying about screws or rules or if someone's coming to check on me. When I was at the hostel, if I was in on my own, or if I was on the beat or whatever, I used to walk over to the hill on the Forest Recreation Ground just near the hostel and sit there, night or day, and smoke a spliff to myself and watch men playing football, or the Asian lads playing cricket on the park-and-ride. If it was night time I'd watch crack-heads, rent-boys, punters, and drunks on their way home, or mucking about, doing what they were doing. None of them could see me and sometimes it felt dangerous. The Forest is sometimes a dodgy place to be and it was fresh to sit and blaze a joint and not care.

That's how I was: cotched in a prison cell blazing a jay like I was on the out. I gave Shanice twos and she smoked it near the window. We were chatting and having a laugh.

Inside I was sad about the way Crawley had gone on. Fucking her with my fingers was exciting and the best sex I'd given another person, even though I din't get an orgasm out of it. I was stretched on my bed, wounded about it, feeling stoned and wondering if Crawley was gonna carry on being fuckeries when I came back from court with a sentence. Maybe she was thinking it wun't matter 'cause I'd be going onto another wing, a different unit for convicted girls. I wanted her to want me, though. I did, I really did. I wasn't only thinking about court and what sentence I was gonna get. I din't wanna be in prison. I wanted to be free and somehow get to college and do a music course and get people to hear my rapping and record a CD and all that, get away from all the crap and crime. If I was gonna do more time I wanted Crawley with me. Things wun't be as bad then. I was scared of getting a large sentence and I was biting ma nails all the while and when I was on my bunk, not talking or looking at Shanice, I had little tears in my eyes.

My bruises were still sore. The top of my legs looked like they'd been sprayed brown, black and blue with paint. Still, I got stoned that night, and din't get no piss tests or stress from the screws.

I remember the next day or the day after, I got a letter that made me cry my eyes out. Shanice was out at education classes all afternoon and I was probably on my bed reading a book or a magazine or just chilling. The screws used to shove the mail under the cell door at about three o'clock each day. I jumped up when I heard the sound of the envelope coming under the door. I grabbed the letter, like a normal looking white envelope, but din't recognise the writing at all. Usually I could tell if it was from my mum or Boo Boo Girl, 'cause they'd sent me a couple of letters since I'd been inside, but this one was from someone who'd not written before. It was Rachel Robbins, one of my best mates from school who I used to knock about with and stay with at her house in Sherwood. I cried because of the way Rachel said she was shocked that I was in prison, how everyone we knew from school couldn't believe it, and that she was gutted thinking about me being alone and not free to get on with my life like all my old mates were. My tears were dripping onto her letter. She told me about college and working part time and going out at weekends and having holidays abroad and getting qualified and ready to go to university and all that. There was me sat in a stinking prison with hundreds of other girls, and my life was down the pan and messed up big time, and I wished I could be back with Rachel Robbins and all the old crew from school. I used to think living in the hostel and blazing draw all day was proper like, well freedom I suppose, that's what I saw it as. Obviously what Rachel was doing was better and more like having power in life. She'd be set up, able to live nice and I'd just be plodding along and not sorting myself out and living like a druggy and wasting my talent.

Rachel reminded me of one time in art class when Mrs Clarke asked me to perform one of my raps for the rest of the class. I stood up on the table and everyone clapped along to make a beat and I did one of my raps and every single girl and boy loved it and cheered and bigged me up. It felt like I was a pop star or summat, people were coming up to me for time after bigging me up and loving it, and the boys who were into rapping and beat boxing were bigging me up and saying I had skill. That's when I knew I wanted to be a famous white girl rapper, as good as the boys, and even better than some of 'em, but I wan't gonna get nowhere riding jail time all my life.

I needed to fix up, that's what they say when you need to get ya shit together and get somewhere in life. I din't wanna be like Di and DD and loads of girls like them; in and out of jail, criminal records long as ote; can't get a good job, known by the feds; dissed by old friends for being dodgy. I din't wanna end up like Shanice repping a street gang and looking to stay true to it till I died or got lifed off. That life was in me, there's no doubt about it. I could've killed Henley, if my knife had gone in a different part of his body, I'd have been on a murder charge. I'd have been like Natty, doing years on remand and then getting slammed with a twenty-five year sentence. I'll be forty years old when Natty gets out, that's even if she gets out: they might never let her out. I din't want nobody messing with me and I wanted peeps to know they couldn't take the mick, but I wanted a better life. I din't wanna be just another street girl, working the beat 'cause it's easy, risking my life to keep blazing. I din't want that crap if I had talent, proper skills that could give me a good life and get me out of the rough area, and stop me from being poor. Deep down I wished to be a college girl, hanging around with normal lads and girls, not wanna-be gangsters or rude-boys, or dick-heads and bullies. I'd been there and done that. I wanted to be with people who wanted to sing and rap and record music in proper studios and produce CD's and try and get on the radio and in the papers. I din't wanna be looking over my shoulder, carrying tools, and risking battering someone or getting battered, raped on the beat, or dying from a drug overdose.

I had a bad start in life from being poor and not being what's-it-called? Stable and secure. I wasn't living stable and secure like kids should be. Not just me, my sisters an' all. And most people don't change from that life. You grow up poor, you have a shit life, you go without, and it's normal; and then you stay like that and that's the way it goes. You end up praying to win the lottery, or meet some rich guy who will pay for you to have a holiday and a car and a decent life and that's about it. Fuck that. I wanted summat bigger and better than that.

I wan't gonna be sitting in a pub like an alcoholic, caning pints and telling all the other piss-heads that I coulda been famous, or that I was a great rapper back in the day and they'd be like, *well why din't ya do it?* I'd be gulping my drink and going, *I dunno.* They probably wun't even believe me. That's a nightmare life as far as I'm concerned and I din't wanna go out like that. I needed to change my ways for definite. I could've gone on and done enough crime and done more jail time and probably raised a bit of cash here and there. Or I could sit in the park or in the pub all day pissing my life away. Or I could fix up and try and make something of my life. It's obvious what to choose when ya look at it like that, but believe me, most people will choose crime and blazing because they ain't got it in 'em to change their ways. I din't have any excuses, though. I needed to get my sentence done and come out the other end stronger then when I first went in.

I was shitting myself the day before I went to court, I couldn't eat or stop thinking about what I was gonna get. I saw Crawley a couple of times and she was safe and acting all nice, like we were all good. I went along with it, because I wanted to be mates with her and still liked her. She was asking me if I liked what we did and if I enjoy it. We snogged once in the bogs the night before I went to court and she had her hands down my knickers and she was rubbing me up a bit which felt nice and made me think she was gonna fuck me eventually. It felt wicked to be with her in that way. I acted like I wan't bothered about court, like I was some gangster-bitch or summat, but that was all fake and fronting, 'cause I was as nervous as a bastard, I'm telling ya.

28 Smoke

On the morning I was in court the screws came to collect me at half-seven to take me and my little plastic bag of prop' to the reception.

I'd already been up since about six o'clock, walking up and down in the cell in my socks, making sure I din't wake Shanice, worrying about what was gonna happen. My stomach felt weird, kind of like when I'm on the rag, but not so much pain. Like butterflies, except it was tighter.

Before they take you on the sweat-box you have to sit in this big room that stinks, with stains all on the floor and walls, and it's full of girls who are going to different courts around the country. The place was full of fag smoke and noise from the chatting, laughing, and shouting. The room was like a canteen hall, with grubby tables and metal chairs bolted down, a TV on the wall in the corner that no fucker could hear 'cause of the noise, and a hatch at one end with a screw and a prisoner serving eggs and slices of dry toast for breakfast. There was a queue of girls waiting to get theirs, but I din't fancy dry toast, and there's no way I woulda got the egg down. I went and sat down with my stuff and got out a roll-up.

One of the fattest girls I've ever seen in my life, she was sat at a table near me, turned around and asked for twos. I nodded yeah, but din't say ote. I couldn't be arsed to start talking to people. I was too busy trying to stop myself from shaking and being bummy. There musta been about a hundred girls in that smelly room. One or two of 'em were going home. That's where ya had to wait to be released, but they had to wait till all the court-heads were out of there first. I recognised a couple of girls, but I just nodded, smiled and said, 'Safe.'

I saved the fat girl twos, and she said thank-you, and

the other girls on her table begged her for three's and four's and last drags. Prisoners are like flies around dog shit when it comes to stuff like tobacco and drugs and munchies and whatever. You pull out a burn and everyone's on ya case, and it's mainly people you don't know. Imagine you were walking down the street, minding your own business, as free as ya like, and you sparked up; you wun't have a stranger coming up and going, *gis twos on that?* And another random guy or someone going, *and can I have three's?* In jail, as soon as you've got something, everyone else wants a piece of it.

I din't even hear the screw shouting me.

The fat girl turned.

'That's you in't it, Walters?'

I goes, 'Yeah.' I din't know how she knew me, I'd never spoke to her before then.

The fat girl goes, 'They're calling ya.' She pointed towards a door at the other side of the room. There was a bloke screw stood there. He shouted my name again, but he wan't looking at me, he was looking all over the place.

I stood up and lifted up my hand a bit to the show him I was coming. All he said was: 'Get a move on.'

As I walked with my bag of stuff through the room, a few girls said, 'Eh, up.' I got to the door: the screw took my bag and moved out the way to let me go through.

I went into a little room, like a changing room, with benches and compartments where you get changed and searched. There were two women screws - one was like a butch dyke and the other was skinny with long blond hair - stood next to the compartments, with blue plastic gloves on their hands. The screw who shouted me into the room chucked my little bag to the screw behind the hatch and they started to search through it. It was only a few toiletries, letters, a pack of cards, some pens and pencils, and shit like that. Actually, it was all I had in the world, but only the letters were important to me. The butch dyke screw called me over and told me to walk into the cubicle and get naked. It was about my third or fourth strip search, so I was getting used to people gawping at my naked body.

The skinny blonde went, 'Give me your shoes, please.' I took 'em off and passed them to her. She looked inside and put her hands in them and checked behind the tongue and on the sides. She passed them back to the butch screw and she put them down on the floor.

Then she asked for my socks. I slipped them off and she turned them inside out and passed them to the dyke. Next it was tracksuit bottoms, my knickers, and then I had to squat, which is probably the most embarrassing part of the search, 'cause ya bits are there like you're having a piss or summat and for all to see. They both looked at my fanny as I went down. I had to take off my top and my bra, lift up my breasts, which aren't massive anyway, stick my hands in the air, and turn around. The butch one passed me a black box that she got from the screws behind the hatch, and it had my jeans and top and bra and knickers I wore when I first went in. It was a blue, like dark blue, top with three white stripes down the arms, a pair of black jeans, white knickers and bra, white socks. The skinny screw said, 'Get dressed and go through there,' pointing at a door to the side. I din't say anything, but I pulled the brown curtains across to get a little privacy. I quickly dressed and wrinkled my nose 'cause the clothes were a bit fusty from being in that box weeks without being washed.

When I came out, another girl was getting strip-searched in the next cubicle. I walked through the door that the screw showed me and it was another room full of girls. Each one was dressed in their fusty, sweaty tracksuits and jeans and knickers that had been manky in their property boxes. The room had benches running all around the sides and girls were sat in every space. The air was full of fag smoke and stank of sweat and piss. I don't know how anybody would've had time to wee in there, but it still stunk like that. I don't think there was a place in the jail that din't smell of something nasty or chemical. There was nowhere to sit, so I stayed standing with a dozen other girls. I din't look at any of them; there was lots of talking and laughing, but I din't want anybody to chat to me.

Girls were being called through a door at the other side of where I came in and after a minute or three of standing about I got a space on a bench. I squeezed between two girls I kind of knew from my wing. I can't remember their names. We got chatting about what courts we were going to and what we were gonna get and what Judges we had and all the shit that prisoners always talk about.

The lass on my left had black hair in a ponytail and big scabs on her lips and hands. Proper skag-head scabs. I din't even wanna look at her. Her trainers were battered with holes in. She was from Leicester and was up for theft from a shop, basically shoplifting to feed her habit. The girl on my right was from some bumpkin place outside of Leicester and she had dark hair as well, but was pretty and din't look like a brown-head. I think she was up for shoplifting as well, I can't remember, but it was something minor like that. You wun't believe how many girls and women are in jail for nicking from shops. I couldn't even believe Judges would bother to waste every fucker's time sending them to jail for a month here or a month there. Most of 'em had kids as well, so it splits up the family. The worst crime in the world ain't nicking from shops, I'll tell ya that.

After a couple of minutes chatting to the shoplifters I was called through the door and into the main reception where there's a big desk with a couple of screws behind it and computers on it. There was a Group 4 security guy with handcuffs and a metal detector. I had to sign at the big desk for my property that had already been taken onto the sweatbox, the bus that takes us to court. The Group 4 guy moved the metal detector all around my arse, fanny, hair, and legs and arms to make sure I din't have weapons or tools stashed. If you know what you're doing you can escape from sweatboxes, so they're always checking that no-one's trying it on.

The Group 4 bloke handcuffed my left wrist to his

right one, walked me out of reception and into the bright sunny day to get on the bus.

The reason prison and court buses are called sweatboxes is because they're tiny spaces they make you sit locked in. Imagine if you're sitting in a small plastic chair and you moved your elbows out, like you were tryna do a chicken impression, well you're touching the sides with them and you can't stretch your feet out like you would if you were on a train or plain. You're locked in the space, and it's cramped, and the plastic seat is hard on ya bum and back, and it stinks of sweat and farts and piss and god knows what else. It's like a coffin, but for sitting inside instead of lying. Imagine you have to spend an hour or two in one, and that's why everyone calls it the sweatbox.

I din't sit down straight away. I stood up to get ready to look out of the tinted window so I could see the fields, trees, and sunshine; stare at men and women driving their cars to work. That's when being a prisoner does your head in, watching people free, going about their daily lives and probably not even seeing the sweatbox go past with twelve girls locked inside.

Like cattle, or horses or another animal being moved about, and the animals looking out the window thinking, *I wanna be out there, in that place, the place where I eat stuff and run about happy* and it's a field, but it don't know its a field, it just knows it wants to be there. That's what I felt like in the sweatbox. I was desperate to be free.

I stared at the countryside, the morning sunshine, everyone on their way to work, the trains and planes, and the wildlife mooching about, like birds and rabbits and sheep. I even saw a dead fox in the road, all splattered and squashed. I wondered if it had kids waiting at home, starving and crying, not realising they were on their own and their mum was dead.

When the sweatbox started getting closer to Nottingham some of the other girls, the ones who din't get off at Leicester Crown Court, started shouting, 'We're here,' and banging on the doors and windows. They were celebrating, 'cause we were back in the place we were born and raised. I smiled at the noise they were making, but then I got sad about the situation, because the bus was going past places that I knew well and had memories of. We went through Clifton, over the bridge across the Trent, and I saw the rugby field at Wilford where I stood when I was a little girl, watching the fireworks on Bonfire Night, jumping when the big ones exploded. The bus went through part of The Meadows, past the Wickes DIY place, where I got a glimpse of Bosworth school field where we used to sing and dance near the boys playing football, and where my old best mate, Diedre Pykett, split her thumb wide open because we threw stones at a TV left out near the bins and glass flew into her hand. The sweatbox drifted past my old school, Welbeck Primary, and I could see a bit of the concrete playground and park just as we turned towards the train station. I was lonely and wounded.

29 Slammed

My mum was waiting at the court and she was with Boo Boo Girl: we were allowed to see each other for about half an hour before I went up for my sentence. We got lucky really, 'cause they stopped family visits not long after I got my sentence, now no-one can see their friends or family at Nottingham Crown Court. I think that's fucked up, and I don't know why they changed it.

It was the same visiting cubicles I saw my mum in before I was remanded to jail for the first time. It seemed like I'd been in prison for ages, the way that I'd lived all those experiences like shagging Crawley, battering DD, and getting done in by the screws; plus meeting all those different girls and living with murderers and baby killers. My mum din't have a clue what my life inside was like, and she would have cried her eyes out for a month if she knew. Boo Boo din't know it all either, but she did know about the fights with DD and me being down the block. I told her about it in letters.

The first thing my mum said to me from behind the glass was, 'You look pale.'

I laughed, not a big laugh, just a giggle, to try and come across like I din't give a shit and everything was all good.

I goes summat like, 'Well I don't see much sun now!' I could see they were gutted for me, even though they were full of smiles.

Boo Boo looked glamorous. All I was used to were jail-head girls, mostly smack-heads and trolls, all wearing shitty prison clothes and hardly any make up. Looking at Boo Boo's dyed blonde dread locks, flowery pinkish mascara, lip-gloss and lip-stick, and all that, was like seeing some girl in a trendy magazine. Her cleavage was all showing, because she had on a tight white blouse with most of the buttons loose, and she looked sexy. She'd gone for an all white look, with trousers and shoes, probably because it was court and she wanted to look good, and I bet she was swinging heads outside. I was sat in my sweaty top and bottoms and felt like a right tramp, but it was good to see Boo Boo, like she had some of her old self back and wasn't looking so depressed and sad, like she was all those months before. That showed me that people can get over shit in their lives, but it takes time. You just have to struggle on and get stronger and not let shit run you into the ground.

I was proud of Boo Boo for getting better. I don't know what its like to be raped, and I wun't wanna know, but I seen with my own eyes that girls can get over it and have a life again, and smile again, and maybe start to trust again.

As me and my mum chatted about what I'd been doing at Glen Dale, me and Boo Boo held our palms up, my right had and her left hand, and pressed them against the glass like we were boyfriend and girlfriend. My mum want bothered, she was just asking questions.

'What ya been eating?'

'Who's your cell-mate?' Me and Boo kept looking at each other and smiling.

Boo Boo never said anything about why I stabbed Robert Henley, because of what he did to her, she never said thank-you or ote like that, and din't need to. I could tell our friendship was getting stronger, I knew we were gonna be mates for a long time, and know each other's kids, and live down the road from each other, and all that lot. That's what it felt like to me, even in my head. When I was thinking I was gonna be a famous white girl rapper, I imagined coming back for Boo Boo in a limo and taking her to my concerts and spending money on her and showing her the high life and letting her move into my mansion and go everywhere with me.

I asked Boo Boo about people at the hostel, who was gone and who was new. She said Scott had been given his own flat with Kissian sleeping on his sofa, and Martin was still there. That was it from our crew, everyone else had been kicked out or left. Life was moving on. Boo Boo had the biggest room on the top floor, which had a proper kitchen bit inside and a nice carpet, from her massive window she could see out over north Nottingham as far as Bestwood Park and fields around that way. Boo Boo was tryna get on a drama course at Clarenden College, I think she'd already done one, like the low level one, and she wanted to do the next level and get the certificate. I was pleased for her, and I was smiling and saying it was dead good, but inside I was feeling so sad because I know I would have to serve more time before I could have a go at the things I wanted to do. I wanted to cry to my mum, but I had to put on a brave face and act like I was cool and I could handle it.

My mum asked me what sentence I was looking.

'I don't know ma, hopefully not summat big.' She started getting tears in her eyes. I told her I'd be alright, that I could get through it and come out the other end all good and ready to live my life. The truth was I was shitting myself and I was scared like mad.

By rights, the Judge could give me what he wanted, even a life sentence. My solicitor and barrister said I'd had to have a worse record than what I did to get lifed off. I probably would have killed myself if I got a life sentence. People who get life sentences, lifers, I don't know how they get through it. Actually, I do know how, because you just have to get on with it and do your bird, but what I mean is I don't know how they can survive fifteen or twenty-five years being locked in a cell.

The court screws told me I was wanted in court and I finished my visit by telling my mum and Boo Boo Girl that I loved them and saying, 'I'll be alright.' They both waved as I walked away, back to my cell, and I nearly burst out crying just from the sad look on my mum's face.

The cell door locked and I sat there taking deep

breaths and talking out loud, saying shit like, 'I'll get through this,' and 'I've got hope.' I started to shake and my mouth was going dry. I had to start walking backwards and forwards because I din't know what else to do with myself. That's how nervous I was. I was wondering where my solicitor was an' all.

My door opened and a Group 4 screw was stood there with a pair of handcuffs.

'Time for court.'

He cuffed my right wrist to his left one and we walked passed the reception area of the holding cells and went up a couple of flights of stairs to court five. I asked him what Judge it was.

'Judge Bennett.'

'Shit.' I'd heard from other girls that Bennett was a bastard and loved slamming people.

We stood outside a light-brown door for a minute or two, and then we went in; he took the handcuffs off and walked me to the dock. He told me I had to stand up when the Judge came in. I nodded and sat down.

The court room was modern looking, quite bright with light walls and a clean carpet covering the floor. Straight ahead from where I sat was the Judge's bench, higher up than everything else. In front of that were smaller desks and benches where a grey-haired woman sat in front of a type-writer. She was waiting to type up everything that was said. In front of her little desk was a long bench and that's where the prosecution barrister and my barrister were watching with all their paper work spread out.

The prosecution was a small guy with black hair and black glasses and he had on one of them black robes and daft wigs. He turned 'round and had a proper look at me. He had a little squirrel face and I remembered from the trial that he had a squeaky voice and talked like he was nervous. My barrister, I can't remember his name, was tall and good-looking and was always relaxed and smiley.

My solicitor wan't in court because he was on

another case, but there was a blonde women solicitor representing him, and she had a posh suit on and pointy shoes. She was sitting at the table behind the barrister and near to me. She got up, walked to the dock, and spoke to me through the hole in the thick glass that was there to stop people from doing a runner.

'Sorry that we couldn't speak to you before you were called up,' she said.

'It's okay.'

She went, 'The Judge is reading the reports and then he'll come in and speak for a few minutes, and then we'll give mitigation and then he'll sentence you.'

I knew what the score was so I said, 'Yeah', and sat down again. Before my solicitor went back to her seat she said my barrister would come and see me in the cells. I smiled and nodded because I was too nervous to say ote.

On the right side of the court there was a public bit, the public gallery they call it, and there were random people sat in the chairs looking at me, solicitors and court workers. I din't know any of them. My mum and Boo Boo Girl came in, smiled and waved, and sat near the strangers. I waved back, but then looked away because I din't want Judge Bennett to come in and see me smiling and waving like I was at Goose Fair. I looked at them with my face serious. I was too bummy for smiles.

About a minute went and two more court workers, court clerks, with robes on and with clipboards in their hands, came in and started chatting to the barristers. One of the clerks, a black woman, went up to a door at the back, near the Judge's bench, opened it, popped her head around it, and said summat to someone inside the back room. It must have been the Judge, or one of his joey's, because the next thing ya know the clerk said, 'All rise,' and we stood while Judge Bennett came in and did a little bow and said something I couldn't hear as he sat down.

Everyone else sat. The Judge looked old, like sixty years old or whatever, he had grey hair which I could see under his daft wig, and he had an angry looking face. He looked like a bloke who was always pissed off. When he stared at me I looked down. He had small glasses on the end of his nose and he poked them up to his eyes with his skinny fingers when he was looking at paper-work.

The black woman, court clerk or whatever she was, said a few things to the barristers and then turned around, looked at me, and told me to stand up. She asked my name.

'Stephanie Walters.'

I told her my date of birth and gave my address as the hostel at Waterloo, even though I was still in jail.

The clerk told me to sit down, and the little prosecution guy stood up and was going on to the Judge about how I was found guilty of serious charges and violence that led to injuries on an innocent man, and then he's on about the wounds on Robert Henley and flashing photos of the cuts and stitches and all that, and I'm clocking the Judge and he's still looking well pissed off. He looked at me again and I just looked away. I din't have the guts to hold his stare. The prosecution guy started reading out chunks, all the bad bits, from Robert Henley's statements. I'm not saying he din't have the right to make it ten times worse for me in front of the Judge, but I couldn't believe it when he said he'd rang Glen Dale and found out I smacked DD over the head. My mum looked shocked as well and she started crying, Boo Boo Girl had to put her arm 'round her. He never mentioned the fight with DD or anything, he just said I attacked another inmate with a weapon made out of batteries, and he told the Judge that I'd been down the block. Even my solicitor turned around and had a worried look on her face. I wanted to shout out what the screws had done to me and Zahra, that I got strangled and beat up and pissed on, but they probably wun't have believed me. I could feel tears in my eyes and had to fight not to burst out crying.

When it was my barrister's turn to get up to give my mitigation, the Judge looked like he wan't even interested. Judge Bennett: what a prick.

My barrister's going, 'She's had a tough upbringing in The Meadows area of the city and a very challenging time at a hostel in Radford.' He told the Judge I was sorry for what I did and that prison was hard for me, and that a big sentence wasn't necessary for me to learn my lesson. After he said his bit he sat down and the Judge told me to stand up.

I can't remember all the exact words Bennett said before he sentenced me, but it was stuff like he couldn't believe an intelligent girl like me had gone off the rails and done bad things like the robberies when I was younger, and then stabbing Robert Henley and being rowdy in prison. I was still looking down because I couldn't look in his eyes.

He din't know me; all he knew were bits of paper, B.S. written about me by people who also din't know me. He's spouting off all his big words and I'm thinking, *what's he gonna give me?* My body's shaking like mad and my hands were sweaty and I swear all I could hear was my heart beat pumping in my ears, like when you stand up quick and the blood goes to ya head.

Mum was still crying and rubbing her nose with tissue, and I could tell Boo Boo had tears in her eyes. The strangers in the public gallery were staring at either me or the Judge, or moving their heads to look at him, then me, and then back at him.

The Judge was more pissed off because I'd pleaded not guilty and been found guilty, which was worse. He said that he would've given me less time if I'd have gone guilty when I had the chance and not wasted the courts time, because that cost money. He said he was gonna give me a bit extra for that disrespect. He said I should be ashamed of myself for upsetting my family. He said because Robert Henley feared for his life that made it worse, and he was gonna punish me for that as well. He told me not to think that being a girl would stop him from handing down a long custodial sentence, even for someone who was only seventeen. He handed down the sentence in months, which is normal for Judges to do, but I'm shit with numbers, so I had to look over at Boo Boo who made signs with her hands.

The Judge said, 'That's all, you can go back.' The screw came and put the cuffs back on.

I heard my mum crying out loud and saying something like, 'She's only a girl.'

On the way back to the cells I asked the screw what my sentence was. I still hadn't worked it out.

'You got four-and-a-half years, love,' he said.

'Four-and-a-half?' I asked, shocked.

'Yeah.'

I still felt as if I'd taken loads of speed or coke or summat; like I was tripping out. It was like a dream, like it wan't really happening and I was gonna wake up either in my cell at Glen Dale, or even at the hostel at Waterloo, like they do in films.

The screw locked me in the holding cell and I sat down with my head in my hands. My face was throbbing, like when you start to get a head-ache, and I repeated my sentence.

'Four-and-a-half years.'

I couldn't sit for very long because my heart was going mad, so I stood up and walked in a circle.

Twelve months for the robbery of the credit-card from Robert Henley, twelve months for kidnapping him in the boot of his own car, and thirty months for the stabbing - the section eighteen charge. Four and a half years.

It took me a few minutes to work out how long I had left to serve. I counted the bricks in the cell walls and used them as months and years. Cons had to serve two-thirds of the whole sentence in those days. By using the bricks to help me work it out, I knew I had to do three years before I could get out, meaning I wun't be going home 'till I was twenty years old. I started to get proper tears; I'll tell ya that for nothing. I'd done a couple of months on remand, but I'd lost most of that for fighting DD and smacking her up with the tool. It was like starting fresh with three years. I was gutted, but it din't sink in properly for a couple of months.

A woman Group 4 screw came to the door.

'Your mum and friend are in the visiting room, d' ya wanna see them?'

'Not really.'

I couldn't face my mum and Boo Boo without bawling my eyes out. I knew they'd come and see me at Glen Dale.

'Can I just go back on the bus?' I asked.

'Okay,' the screw said, 'next one's at one.'

*

Liam Rodgers is a 1999 Koestlar Award winner and has had material screened on Channel 4 and the Web. Recently he was a finalist in the QUAD Short Film Commission with his short script, *Redwood Runner*.

Having changed his own life around from one of crime, prison and drug abuse during his teenage years and one relapse during adulthood, Liam has concentrated his efforts into producing many dozens of songs, stories and pieces of art. He has been in bands, ran a small production company, been a youth-worker, a street busker, a tree-protestor, a cook and more!

Liam is thirty-four, has two children, Niamh and Jupiter, and currently lives in Derby with his partner, Star.

This book is also dedicated to many people, some of whom are sadly no longer with us and it is those I shall mention first: Martin, Amy the Rocker, Jon Bennell, Philip Heinemann, Ryan 'The Small King' Michael Freestone Rodgers, and our recently departed and beloved cousin, brother and father, son and friend, Brice Veevers. Always remembered.

To those still breathing: All my roines and scroines, Stamina guys (KB, LS, JH, Tyrone, E.B., etc) especially Liam 'Leds' + Laura O'Brien, Mark 'Garvey' O'Brien, Ruben and Aidy, Tristan 'Tray' Young and Joshua, Aaron 'Azzy-Dee' Calladine, Kim and their lovely girls, No5, the Waterloo Cru, (Dean, Jay, Louis, Eddie, etc) my brothers Jade and Sebastian (Sebba Esparr) and my Nottingham aunties, Elaine 'Lainey' Veevers, Laura, Sue, Jacky and Annetta and cousins Chloe, Kerry, Rowan, Jacko, Gabsy, RA, Nico, Sarah and Luke, Amy, Jo and Alex and Django the dog! My ma and pa, Paula and Breg, and in Ireland, to Wendy and my precious brothers and sisters: Pat, Maeve, Erin and Calum, Alice and their wonderful children, my nieces and nephews, including Faye, Sydney, Jake, Amber, Ruby and the twins. Also to Terrence Green, Micah Green and Matthew Pyckett: friends and fellow authors and poets. Not forgetting Jared Wilson, especially for support when times were tough, visits and kind words and Tim Evans + Ben Cohen for similar reasons. Pete Waller. Stefan Scally and all my Mokshah bandmates, Josh Crofts, Natasa Luckovic, Claudia-from-Italy, Jules Schofield, Declan Green. Vinolent. Tru Livety Camp, Kasm, A.Z., Sebba Esparr, Phasix, Shad-Da-Farda & Nemo Shaw: *on this rocky road!* The Magic Hat Rainbow Circle, all the hippies, flakey, spikey, fluffy or otherwise. All the anarchos, from hither-to-thither. Helen Wilson, for sound advice. To Janet and Ruth, for all the memories, (to name a few: parachuting, barn-house gimp mask, window diving, cat-that-likes-the-light-and-runs-away, etc!) sisters from another mother! All the MM…Deli posse and of course Martin Derbyshire, from up north.

All my love and light, hugs and kisses, hand shakes and fist bumps, high-fives and back-slaps…Liam x

Feel free to contact me for any reason:
liam-777@live.co.uk
Facebook: Dogknife &/or Liam Rodgers
Twitter: @777Leds